Blood Kin,
A Savannah Story

Blood Kin,
A Savannah Story

Robert T.S. Mickles, Sr.
with a foreword by Aberjhani

iUniverse, Inc.

New York Lincoln Shanghai

Blood Kin, A Savannah Story

iUniverse books may be ordered through booksellers or by contacting:

iUniverse
2021 Pine Lake Road, Suite 100
Lincoln, NE 68512
www.iuniverse.com
1-800-Authors (1-800-288-4677)

This is a work of fiction. All of the characters, names, incidents, organizations, and dialogue in this novel are either the products of the author's imagination or are used fictitiously.

ISBN: 978-0-595-45129-6 (pbk)
ISBN: 978-0-595-89441-3 (ebk)

Printed in the United States of America

To my children, my grandchildren, and the generations that follow.

Foreword

As this book goes into publication, the city of Savannah is involved in the process of reinterpreting the significance, artifacts, and impact of slavery that was practiced here during the 1700s and 1800s. This reinterpretation is not so much about dredging up the pains and shames of an inglorious past as it is about setting straight the historical record of people who lived daily through "the peculiar institution of slavery." As much as facts tell us about specific events and practices in history, they rarely give us the full story of the human hearts beating in the shadows of those events.

Blood Kin is a story of those human hearts as told by Robert T.S. Mickles, Sr., the great-grandson of former slaves on his father's side of his family and a descendant of Portuguese slave traders on his mother's side. Born in Savannah, Georgia, in 1953, Mickles moved with his family to Washington D.C. just three years later. Growing up in Washington, he knew nothing about his deeper southern roots. That changed when he turned thirteen years old and his mother sent him back to Savannah to live with his father in the city's historic community of Sandfly.

In Savannah, his grandmother, Mrs. Beulah Tremble, told him stories of what life had been like for slaves in the region. Having been born in 1888, first-hand accounts of slavery were typical subjects of conversation while she grew up herself. She kept and shared the knowledge passed on to her until her death at the age of 100 in 1988. Mickles recalls that many of her stories were about harsh times, but a lot were about days of memorable joy. In addition to his grandmother, many others shared their stories with Mickles throughout his teen years, entrusting to him a rare treasury of valuable folk history.

With the legacy of his grandmother's stories and his community's history, Mickles stepped behind Savannah's fabled "moss curtain" to reveal an original literary vision of human beings discovering their deepest humanity in the midst of war, racial oppression, individual fear, and individual hope. Although Savannah for a period was a major location for the import and sale of slaves, Mickles shows how it was also a place where the line between those who were "free" and those who were enslaved was sometimes a bit more relaxed than in many rural areas of the South.

This is not to say that the author excuses an institution ultimately responsible for the death of untold millions or that he views slavery through proverbial rose-colored glasses. It is, however, to say that he is willing to examine the cracks and crevices of history in order to tell a story others might not be willing—or even able, for that matter—to tell. It is the story of how Blacks and Whites stumbled across the dividing lines of race and slavery only to discover that each was as flawed, needy, and human as the other.

Above all, Mickles provides us with an insightful novel of how our sense of humanity preserves itself when assaulted with the degradation of denial, shame, and physical brutality. His *Blood Kin* is a story that retrieves dignity from the trash pile of disgrace and restores it to a place of honor and value. It is one with which many can identify and which, quite possibly, all should embrace.

Author-Poet Aberjhani
author of *The Harlem Renaissance Way Down South*
April 2007

PROLOGUE

Some stories need to be told, and then again some don't. They need to be told so that we never forget. It's up to us to choose whether we believe them or not. This is one that you may not believe. I guess you would have to have been there, and if I hadn't been, then I probably wouldn't have believed it myself. I don't have proof that I've been here before and there is no proof that I haven't. That's just a feeling I get. Like when you walk down a dark street at night and the hair stands up on the back of your neck. I myself don't know if people live more than one lifetime. Maybe you do, and then again maybe you don't. It doesn't really matter. All that matters is that this story needs to be told. The world needs to hear what we have to say. We need to tell our stories.

CHAPTER 1

▼

On July the 6th in the summer of 1844, seventeen years before what we called in the South "The War Between The States," but what history would come to describe as the Civil War, two baby boys were born. They came into this world just hours apart. One of the boys was black, and the other white.

On Woodloe Plantation, the two began their lives in the very heart of the South near Savannah, Georgia. This fact, later in their lives would become their undoing or maybe their salvation. It depends on how you look at it. The two boys were fed from the same breast, the breast of a woman named Ada, who had given birth to only one of the boys. The mother of the child she named Robert, Ada fed her own son last. It was the other child, Master Jones' son, Lew, who drank from her breast first. His mother, the master's wife, said that she didn't have milk to give her son. For this reason, Ada became his nursemaid. She and her newborn son Robert were slaves who both belonged to Master Jones.

Their master was a tall soft-spoken man who, like his father before him, had been born on Woodloe Plantation. The master owned forty acres of land and ninety-three slaves. He knew each one of them by his or her name. Some of them he had known since he himself was a young man. Master Jones treated his slaves well. To him they were like a part of his family, they were Jones' slaves. He took great pride in this and in the fact that he had never taken a whip to any one of them. Slaves were beaten nearly every day on other plantations, but he never had to beat anyone on Woodloe. If someone did something wrong, and that didn't happen often, Master Jones would take away half a day on Sunday. This meant that all the slaves would have to work for half of that day. On the plantation, Sunday was the only day off and every slave looked forward to this. It worked for

Master Jones just as it had worked for his father. He made lots of money and everyone was happy, the master, his wife, their son, and all his slaves lived good lives.

The two boys, Robert and Lew, grew and played together in Ada's cabin. They became inseparable as the years passed. For some unknown reason the two of them didn't care for, nor wanted to play with the other children on the plantation. They were just fine playing amongst themselves. They had each other and seemed satisfied with that. They enjoyed competing with each other to see which was growing the tallest, which could run the fastest, which could throw a rock the farthest. There was always a reason for competition, and they loved it.

At the age of five, Lew's father took him to a nearby schoolhouse for the first time. There, he saw other white children ranging from age five to fifteen. He had seen some of them before when he had gone on trips into town with his father, but had never spoken to any of them. With his greenish-blue eyes as wide as all outdoors, a smile that reached from ear to ear, deep dimpled chin, and slender face, Lew looked around the big room. It had a black slate board in the front, and a big desk about two feet in front of it. Sitting at the desk was Mr. Wallace, the school's headmaster. A wood-burning stove sat in the corner in the back of the room and ten rows of five small desks filled the center of the room. Lew counted fifty desks, and he slowly walked to the front of the class. He noticed that a desk in the front of the classroom was empty. As he walked towards it, he also noticed there were no slaves in the room. Where was his friend Robert? Why hadn't Ada brought him to the schoolhouse, he wondered to himself. Lew sat at the desk and raised his hand the way his father had told him to as they rode to the school that morning.

"Yes?" asked Mr. Wallace.

He was a tall skinny man in a black suit and white shirt. He wore little round eyeglasses and peeped over the top of them. Lew stood up near his desk and in a loud voice asked, "Where are the slaves, why didn't they come to school today?"

The class erupted with laughter. Lew looked around as he wondered what was so funny.

"Niggers don't go to school, they aren't allowed to learn," Mr. Wallace replied. "And to quote Oliver Heford, 'A man is known by the silence he keeps.'"

This was Lew's first lesson at the schoolhouse, and a hard one for him. Once he learned it, Lew kept quiet and never asked another question. In spite of this or maybe because of this the young Lew excelled. He learned to read and he read every book that he could get his hands on. He enjoyed the way that books could take him to places he had never been, and how they introduced him to people he had never seen. In his books, he could spend hours away from those children that had laughed at him his first day of school. Sometimes after he had finished reading a book he would pretend that he was his teacher, Mr. Wallace. He would pretend to look over the top of his little round glasses asking the children questions about the book that he had just read.

Lew became one of the top students in his class after only a few years in school and would remain one of the top students until graduating. When he could, Lew would share his lessons with Robert at the end of a school day. It didn't matter to him that he could get into trouble for this, or even worst, that he could get Robert into trouble. That was the last thing he ever wanted to do. After all, Robert was his best friend. The two of them knew not to let anyone know what they were doing, not even Ada, the woman that Lew looked to as his second mother. The two boys took to heart Lew's first lesson from school: "A man is known by the silence he keeps." For Robert's lessons, the two of them would go to an open field of wildflowers filled with tall green grass, yellow dandelions, white milkweed blossoms, orange marigolds, and lots of other flowers growing all around. There, they would sit in the middle of the field where no one could hear them, then Lew would tell Robert about that day's lesson. Robert knew people said slaves weren't supposed to learn, but just like Lew, he enjoyed learning. His classroom was in the fields, in the woods, and on the banks of Moon River, near the plantation.

Robert was five years old, tall and slender with hazel-colored eyes and curly black hair, when Ada took him to see Old Jordan, the slave who would be Robert's teacher. Old Jordan, known as a storyteller, was about sixty years old. He had been born on Woodloe Plantation, as had his father before him. Jordan knew everything about the plantation, and he began to teach Robert the things that he knew. He taught the wide-eyed boy about plants, trees, animals, the land, and the river. Robert felt as if Old Jordan was the smartest man he had ever met, maybe the smartest in the whole world. He wanted to learn everything the old man had to teach. Some days, Old Jordan would tell Robert, "That enough, no more questions. Boy, you know that I'm an old man, and you are about to wear me out." But deep in his heart, he enjoyed spending time with Robert. He enjoyed the questions. He knew that Robert was a bright young man and would remember the things that he had been taught. Robert couldn't wait to share them with his friend Lew. He would share with him how to make traps, and how to kill and be aware of snakes when working in the rice and cane fields without getting bitten. He told Lew how certain plants could be used to heal sickness, and how by watching what the animals ate, you could learn what you could safely eat.

They both became very good at what they did. And Master Jones seemed as though he took pride in both boys. He took pride in Lew for his mastery of books and penmanship, and in Robert for his skills as a top field hand. "Two fine gentlemen," Master Jones would say to himself when thinking about the boys. "Two fine gentlemen."

Although the two boys grew up on the same plantation, they often felt as if they lived worlds apart. The fact that one was a slave and the other the master's son was something Lew sometimes forgot, or just didn't want to remember.

Robert's mother Ada had no family except him on the plantation. Her mother had died in childbirth while bringing her into the world. Her father had died about a year before Robert was born. Ada was a tall dark-skinned woman with big brown eyes that seemed to draw you into them. She had long curly hair as black as the darkest night, big deep dimples in her cheeks, and long firm legs. Instead of working in the field with most of the other slaves, she worked in the white mansion that all the slaves called the big house, where the Jones family lived. They called the mansion the big house because it had a top and bottom floor, two large columns on the long front porch, large wide doors, and beautiful windows on both floors. The slaves lived in small cabins with no more than one or two rooms.

Ada had started working in the big house at the age of six. She cooked, cleaned, and did whatever Mrs. Jones told her to do. She had done the same job for twenty years, taking only two days off that she could remember, on the day she gave birth to Robert and on the day her father died. Except for then, she had put up with Mrs. Jones day in and day out.

Mrs. Jones was a pale sickly looking woman who weighed about ninety-eight pounds on a good day. She had a thin face with blue eyes, and long blonde hair. She was a very hard person to please and never seemed to be happy. However, Ada had to put up with her for most of her life. She knew how to satisfy Mrs. Jones most of the time. She did this by just saying, "Yes'm ma'am," in her soft voice and smiling as she looked down at the floor in front of her. Ada would never look at Mrs. Jones' face when she spoke to her. She never looked at those cold sickly blue eyes of Mrs. Jones. For Mrs. Jones seemed to like Ada to act that way. She in her own words "could not, and would not tolerate no uppity nigger."

But Ada was no uppity person. Still, Mrs. Jones didn't care much for her, but she knew that Master Jones enjoyed having Ada around. Ada knew them both well. She knew just what to do, and how to do it. She never had to be told. It was as if she could read their minds. Mrs. Jones knew that if she said anything about not liking Ada, Master Jones wouldn't be pleased, and she couldn't risk that. The price that she would have to pay was a little bit too high. After all, this was the South, and a good southern wife never questioned her husband. Although, deep down inside past those blue eyes, down in her very soul, she knew that Master Jones had a liking for Ada. She also knew that for years he had been with her on the nights when he said that he was going for walks to check the plantation. Nevertheless, this was never talked about, nor was it Mrs. Jones' place to ask him about it. Still, it was like a thorn in her side, and she hated Ada for being there. Mrs. Jones knew that Master Jones loved her and that she could get her husband to do almost anything that she wanted him to do, anything except leave Ada alone. But that's just the way things were done in the South.

One thing Mrs. Jones wouldn't do was let Ada's son Robert enter her house. This was the only way that she thought she could hurt Ada. She had to hurt Ada because she herself was hurting inside. She knew Master Jones had to agree so she said, "A house nigger is a house nigger and a field nigger is a field nigger, and field niggers don't belong in the big house." After all, Robert was a field hand, so she won. She had found her way to hurt Ada, but Ada knew the real reason why Mrs. Jones wasn't going to allow Robert in the big house. It was a fact that all the slaves on Woodloe knew but never spoke about. For they all knew too well that to make the master or his wife angry could cause you to be sold off. There were surely a lot worse places than Woodloe Plantation.

The fact that Robert couldn't go inside of the big house didn't matter much to him. As he grew older and spent more time working in the fields, he would say that Ada spent enough time inside that house for the both of them. Besides, the plantation was big enough for Robert, from its stone arched gate to its long dirt road with giant oak trees on both sides leading to the big house. The trees stood like ever-present watchmen, watching over whoever came and went. He also enjoyed the muddy banks of Moon River with its salty smell and soft marsh grass that swayed in the gentle breezes that came from the east. He took pleasure in the rice paddies and the sugarcane fields where Old Jordan taught him to plant and plow. And he looked forward to those times in the field of wildflowers where he and Lew would spend hours talking and sharing what they had learned over the years. Yes, Robert had quite enough to content himself with besides worrying about going inside the big house.

Besides, Old Jordan kept Robert pretty busy both working and learning. He never forgot that first day he met Old Jordan when he was five years old. There was one when Old Jordan told him to get four eggs from the chicken coup and an old piece of rag. Old Jordan took the rag and put it in a bucket of water. Then he placed the four eggs in the wet rag and wrapped them up. He put the whole thing in the ashes of the fire from the night before and walked away. Later, they returned to the ashes. Old Jordan pulled the rag from under them and unwrapped it. He looked at Robert's almond shaped hazel eyes, smiled, and said, "Here boy." The eggs he placed in his hands turned out to be two of the best boiled eggs that Robert ever ate in his life. On another day, Old Jordan showed him how to cook fish or dry out peanuts by placing them on the roof of the house, under the heat of the sun. Yes, Old Jordan was one smart old soul and Robert was always happy to learn everything he had to teach him.

In fact, to Robert, Old Jordan was more like a father than a teacher. The father he had never known. The one he could never get any answers about. Even Ada wouldn't tell him a thing about his father. Robert wondered if he was dead, or had he run away? He had heard about runaway slaves who were killed trying to get away. Is that what happened to his father? Why would anyone run away from Woodloe, unless the master was about to sell him off? Still, no answers from his mother. She would only say, "Pray and God will bless you. Leave it in the hands of the Lord." So Robert just let it go. Like most of the things on Woodloe Plantation, it didn't matter much.

CHAPTER 2

▼

In the summer of 1856 when Lew and Robert turned twelve years old, they were playing along a ditched bank that led to the river. The two were jumping, pushing each other, and having a great time when Lew decided to jump across the ditch. He ran about five feet forward then leaped across. He landed just short of the edge of the ditch. Lew noticed that his hand was on top of something.

"Oh my God," he shouted, "a moccasin! My hand is on the head of a water moccasin!"

He knew he couldn't move his hand. If he did, the poisonous reptile would bite him for sure. He looked around for other snakes.

"Good, I don't see any more," he said to himself.

Seeing what had just happened, Robert grabbed a forked tree limb, and jumped to the other side of the ditch. He stuck the forked limb deep in the ground on top of the snake's head next to Lew's hand, pinning it down so it couldn't move.

"You can pick up your hand now," Robert said.

Lew replied, "Are you sure?"

"Just be sure to do it fast and let's go unless you're planning on being here all day, but that's up to you," Robert said as he walked away.

Lew slowly removed his hand without being bitten by the snake. He jumped up and ran to where Robert was walking.

"Boy was I scared," Lew said in a low voice as Robert pushed him to one side.

"You looked like it", said Robert, "and I told you to move your hand fast, not slow."

They both laughed and walked towards home. As they got close to the big house, Robert turned to go to the slave quarters, and Lew followed.

"What's wrong Lew?" Robert asked.

"Robert, you just saved my life, do you know that?"

"Boy, stop being so silly Lew, you would have done the same thing for me."

But Lew didn't know if he could have, because he had a secret. He was afraid of snakes. Lew turned and walked towards the big house as tears fell from his greenish-blue eyes.

"See you tomorrow," Robert shouted as he went into his house.

The cabin he shared with his mother was mostly a large single room with a small area set up for their kitchen, a padded pallet for him, and a single bed for her on opposite sides of the room. Hanging from a rope was a quilt that they used like a curtain whenever one of them needed privacy. There was no one inside when Robert entered his home because Ada was still working at the big house. She would have to serve supper and wash the dishes before she could leave. Every day Ada would be in that house from before the sun came up until long after it had set. When she came home she would have to wash the clothes that she wore to work. These consisted of a long black skirt, white blouse, and a white apron. She had two of each, so one had to be washed every evening for the next day.

Robert always made sure that he got the wash water ready for his mother, one pot of it cold, and one hot. The only good thing about his mother working late was that Ada would bring Robert the sweets and meats left over from that night's supper. Robert enjoyed this and would wait up for Ada every evening. That night, when he heard her coming, he ran to the door and opened it, ready to look inside her apron for his treat. Ada handed him the apron and sat down on the side of her bed. He reached in the apron's pocket and pulled out a heavy slice of cake.

"You a hero now, hey my son?"

Robert looked up from the sweetbread he was eating and with a smile replied, "What are you talking about mama?"

"I'm talking about you boy, saving Lew's life, keeping him from getting bitten by that snake."

"Wasn't nothing," Robert said, and they both laughed.

The next day life on Woodloe Plantation went on as usual. Robert went to the fields to cut the sugarcane they used to make cane syrup and Lew went to his one room schoolhouse for his lessons. Then, about ten o'clock, Master Jones went to the cane fields where Robert was working.

"Robert, come here boy", he said.

Hearing this, Robert ran towards him.

"Yes sir Master Jones," he said as he approached him. "Boy, who makes the best cane syrup in Savannah?"

"We do," replied Robert.

"Well get Old Jordan and the buckboard, load three barrels on it, and let's go sell some," Mater Jones said, his bright hazel eyes shining and his face smiling.

He found Old Jordan sitting in front of a wagon waiting for Master Jones. Robert walked over to the wagon and said, "Morning," then hopped on the back. He sat down on a sack of rice. Old Jordan told Robert the things he should do and not do once they were in town.

"Make sho you always walk just behind Master Jones and don't look no white folks straight in the eye that you don't know. Keep yo' head down and don't go askin' all those questions the way you do. Exceptin' Master Jones and Master Lew, white folks mostly don't like slaves soundin' too smart."

Robert listened carefully to Old Jordan and promised to do as he said. He then looked around and thought that this day couldn't be more beautiful. He thought about the fact that he had never been away from Woodloe. What would it feel like? Would he see his father? Would he finally go past the oak trees and stone arch gate? This would be the first time in his life that he ever left Ada. He started to worry. What if he didn't come back, what would Ada do, who would take care of her? What if he forgot the things Old Jordan had told him and made a mistake? Then he said out loud in a low voice to himself, "I'm just being silly, Master Jones and Old Jordan would never let anything happen to me."

Robert looked over at the big house and thought that for some reason it appeared to be even bigger. He counted the windows: eight downstairs, eight upstairs. Then he counted the shutters: two on each window. He tried to guess how tall the two pillars were on each side of the front porch. He thought he might have the answer just as Master Jones came out of the house. He got into the front of the wagon and said, "Let's be on our way before it gets hot."

Just like that, Old Jordan shook the horse's reins and the wagon took off. Robert felt his heart beating hard in his chest. What was just another trip to town for Master Jones and Old Jordan was a once in a lifetime journey for him. As the wagon rolled slowly down the road leading away from the big house, Robert started counting the oak trees on each side of the road. Then beyond the trees he saw the field of brightly-colored wildflowers where he and Lew spent countless hours talking. Lew was at school by now and Robert wished that he were going with him. That would have been nice, he thought.

He passed by the fields where slaves were busy at work, some of them stopping long enough to wave goodbye. It seemed as if the whole plantation knew he was going to town and they all were making a big deal out of it. Robert waved back at them and smiled. "I guess this is a big deal," he said to himself. His heart stopped beating so hard and he became more relaxed as he watched the squirrels moving through the branches overhead, jumping from one tree to another. Sunlight danced through the leaves and shined on the moss hanging from the limbs. He noticed how green the grass was and how the smell of the saltwater from the ocean filled the air. Then the wagon began to slowly approach the arch that led off the plantation, drawing closer and closer. He looked up at the stone entrance as the wagon rolled under it and a warm feeling came over him. The already big smile on his face grew larger as he sat up and thought about how lucky he was. He couldn't help thinking that all this had something to do with yesterday. It had something to do with not letting Lew get bitten by that snake.

The ride to town took about an hour, but to Robert, the time went much too fast. There was so much to see, and Robert's big, wide hazel eyes could not move fast enough. He kept thinking to himself, "My first time away from Woodloe."

When they reached town, Old Jordan pulled the wagon in front of the farmers market. He and Master Jones got out. Robert just sat on the back of the wagon, frozen, unable to move his legs, just looking around. It was such a big town, with people everywhere. White people and black people that he had never seen before. He wondered if one of these people knew his father, or was his father.

"Robert, you hear me boy?"

The sound of Master Jones' voice brought him back to reality. "Yes sir," he replied.

"Come go with me. Old Jordan can handle the syrup."

Master Jones started walking across the street and Robert remembered to walk a step or two behind him. As they reached the front of the general store, Master Jones handed Robert six pence. Robert looked in his hand then looked at Master Jones.

"Buy yourself something," he said.

Robert had never bought anything in his life.

"Buy something sir?"

"That's right. Go in and pick out something you want. Make sure it don't cost more than what you got then pay your money for it."

He slowly walked around the store, his wide eyes looking at everything: candy and preserves in clean shiny jars, brand new clothing that no one had ever worn before, large bolts of different-colored cloths, and wooden bins filled with different kinds of seed, and others filled with work tools, some that Robert recognized and some he didn't. There was so much in the store to look at. As Robert walked around, two white men came through the door.

"What this nigger doing here?!" one of the men shouted.

"Nigger you got some money?" the other asked.

Robert stopped dead in his tracks and just looked down at the floor. He didn't say a word. After all, he didn't know these men. As he stood there he heard footsteps coming from behind him. Master Jones then said in a loud voice, "He's with me, he's my boy."

The two men laughed, said okay, and went on their way.

Robert shook his head and said to himself, "Some people are just no good." He continued to look around the store. Soon he saw a white head wrap. His mother would love it, he thought, and it only cost two pence of the six pence he had. "That would leave me with four," he said in a low voice. He walked over to the clerk and handed him the wrap.

"I would like to buy this," he said, "how much is it?"

"Two pence," said the clerk.

Robert looked at his money and picked up two pence. Then he stopped and looked at the clerk. Boy did I almost mess up, he thought. He then opened his hand and said, "I can't count, so you have to get it."

"Put the money on the counter," the clerk said. He didn't want to touch Robert's hand, and took the two pence after Robert laid the money down.

Robert knew that if Master Jones was not standing in the store, the clerk would have surely cheated him because everyone knew that slaves couldn't count money. Robert was glad that he hadn't given himself away by letting the clerk know that he could count.

"It don't matter," he thought as he put the wrap in his shirt and the four pence in his pocket.

He walked to the front door, and waited for Master Jones. When Master Jones approached him, he had about four packages. As they walked out the store, he handed one to Robert.

"This is yours," he said.

Robert thanked him and they walked back to the farmers market. As Robert walked, he smiled to himself and thought, Mama sure will be surprised when she sees what I got for her. Master Jones didn't say anything to Robert or Old Jordan on the trip back home. Robert couldn't help but wonder if he had done something wrong. Did Master Jones know that he could count? Was he supposed to give him the money he hadn't spent? Robert didn't know.

When they got back to Woodloe, Old Jordan pulled the wagon in front of the big house. Master Jones got out of the wagon, and went into the house. He never said a word.

"Strange," Robert said to Old Jordan.

"I've seen a lot stranger than that from white folk," Old Jordan replied. "Keeps on livin, that's what you do boy, keeps on livin. Now help me unhitch this wagon, and put up this horse."

As soon as they were done, Robert went home. He put the wrap he had bought for Ada on her bed. He then opened the package that Master Jones had given him. Inside was a new pair of pants and a new shirt. Robert was so happy that he danced around the room. He then put the clothes on his pallet and went outside. He went to get the water for Ada to wash her clothes. Then he got some wood and made a fire to heat the water. After this was done, he went to the field of wildflowers because he knew that Lew would be coming home soon. Robert had to tell him about his day and how he had almost given himself away, but proved that he was too smart for that.

"Be known by silence," he said to himself as he waited.

CHAPTER 3

▼

One pleasant day in the fall of 1860, a cool wind blew from the east all over Woodloe Plantation, rustling the leaves in the giant oak trees and causing the hanging moss to sway lazily back and forth. The residents of the plantation were all involved in their daily work when suddenly, a black carriage pulled by two horses, wet with sweat and breathing hard as if they were about to keel over, came through the stone arch entrance to the plantation. The carriage made its way down the long dirt road and headed for the big house. Not many people came to Woodloe, and no one there had ever seen this carriage before, so everyone within eyeshot of the house stopped what they were doing and watched. They stood where they were, waiting and watching to see who it was that had come for a visit.

The carriage pulled up in front of the big house. The slave riding on the back quickly jumped down almost before the thing came to a stop and opened the door on the side of the carriage facing the house. He then started pulling suitcases from the back of the carriage and placed them by the steps. Then something happened that no one at Woodloe would ever forget. The day that would change Woodloe had come. The change came in the form of the tall wiry looking man riding inside the carriage. He was dressed in black from head to toe. He looked to be about the age of twenty or so. He had cold blue eyes, his mother's eyes, the same ones that no one would dare look into when talking to Mrs. Jones. The young man slowly got out of the carriage. Taking his time, he walked slowly toward the front door as if he owned the place. He stopped just short of the top step and turned to look around. Without saying a word the whole time, the carriage driver just pulled off. The young man continued up the steps.

When he reached the porch the front door flew opened. Mrs. Jones ran out with her arms stretched out, crying at the top of her voice, "My baby, my baby." She grabbed the young man, almost knocking him down as she continuously rocked him in her embrace and cried.

The man pulled her arms down, stepped back, and in a strong voice said, "Mother, it is good to see you again."

Then they turned and they both walked into the house.

"Niggers get my things," the man said as he walked pass two house slaves standing near the front door. The two slaves looked at him, then at each other in surprise. They then looked at Mrs. Jones who said, "You heard him."

Mrs. Jones and the young man walked into the sitting room. Mrs. Jones then introduced the man to her husband. "This is my oldest son Isaac," she said with a smile as wide as all the out doors on her face.

The man reached out his hand and shook Master Jones' hand saying, "Sir, pleased to meet you after all these years."

"Have a seat," Master Jones replied.

Isaac then turned towards his mother and said, "I've brought you a gift." He walked over to her and handed her a small box.

"What is this?" she said.

"Go ahead, open it," Isaac said with a smile on his face.

Mrs. Jones lifted the top of the box and shouted, "My God, look! Pearls! A beautiful pearl necklace!"

Isaac took them from his mother's hand and placed them around her neck. She walked over to a big mirror that hung over the fireplace and stood there, looking at the string of pearls around her neck.

"Thank you son," she said, "thank you."

Lew, hearing all the noise, put down the book he had been reading and left his room. As he walked down the stairs and the big hall that led to the sitting room, he heard his father's voice, and the voice of a stranger. Lew turned and went into the sitting room.

"Who's this?" he said as he looked at the man with his mother's blue eyes.

"He's your brother Isaac," Mrs. Jones replied. "He's your big brother."

The only word Lew could get out of his mouth was, "Brother?" This news came as a big surprise to him. No one had told him that the man was coming, and no one had ever told him that he had a brother. He felt that if he hadn't had a brother in all these years, he didn't need one now. Besides, Robert was the closest thing to a brother he needed.

"Pleased to meet you," Lew said, and walked back out of the room.

All this came as a surprise to most of the slaves on Woodloe Plantation. They knew of the day that Mr. Jones had married the former Miss Thurman, of South Carolina, and brought her home. They remembered the day that Lew was born. They also knew that the Jones had had only one child and that was Lew Jones. Nevertheless, Mrs. Jones had called the stranger her baby. Where did he come from? Who was he? How was it that he had come to visit? How long was he going to be here? Where had he been for all those years? Finally, why did he call the house slaves "niggers" when he walked into the house? Everyone had questions, and everyone knew to keep them amongst themselves as not to anger Master Jones and his wife.

More astonished than the other slaves were the ones who worked in the house because they generally saw most of what went on with the Jones family and lots of times knew more than they wanted to know. That's the way it had often been for Enoch, a very quiet and soft-spoken man. Not much for a lot of talking, more prone to listening, Enoch was a fair-skinned house slave with gray eyes and black wavy hair. He was slim and about five-feet-four-inches tall. Most people thought of him as a kind-hearted person who would do anything for anybody.

Since Enoch's grandfather was said to have been the son of Master Jones' great grandfather, news about unexpected kinfolk like Isaac didn't worry him too much. It did kind of surprise him that the boy was supposed to be Mrs. Jones' son instead of Master Jones'. Both his grandfather and his father had been house slaves like him and they had talked often enough among themselves about the masters having what they called "outside children." But Enoch rarely thought about things like that and almost never talked about them himself. He did his work in the big house, from dusk until midnight, seven days a week, and minded his own business the best he could. Only this new development seemed like it was gonna be everybody's business.

A week would pass before the house slaves and all the others could find out the answers to their questions, but they did. It seemed as though the visitor truly was the son of Mrs. Jones. As fact would have it, she had been married before. Master Jones was her second husband. Her first, was a man named Thurman from Charleston, South Carolina. They had been married for three years when he died from something called consumption. Her son Isaac had lived with his father's parents when Mrs. Jones remarried. He then went off to college and lived on the campus. Now he had come to live with his mother, and to work on Woodloe Plantation.

Isaac said he wanted to get to know his little brother, the brother that he had read about in his mother's letters, but had never met. His little brother was someone he would try to influence to become like him. He wouldn't be that mild mannered boy he had read about. He wouldn't be the one who had grown up playing with Robert and calling the slaves by their names instead of calling them niggers. His little brother would learn that the slaves were like animals and needed to be beaten. He would learn they had to be kept in their place so they wouldn't become uppity.

"Them niggers need to fear us. Without fear we have no control over them," Isaac said. "Me call a nigger by its name, never."

Isaac let everyone know from day one that he would not allow the kind of casual familiarity between his family and the slaves that Master Jones and Lew had permitted. He was to be the master of this domain. He knew that in order to do this, he had to come up with a plan, so he went to Master Jones and told him that he had ways to increase his profits and make Woodloe one of the richest plantations in Savannah. Master Jones told Isaac that Woodloe was doing just fine, and that he didn't need any help controlling his slaves. Mrs. Jones interrupted and said, "Let him try, he's been to college and he knows what he's talking about." She then asked Master Jones, "What will it hurt?"

Master Jones didn't like this, but at the same time he would do anything to keep his wife happy. After all, this was the happiest anyone had seen her in years.

C H A P T E R 4

▼

All the slaves knew something was wrong. They whispered among themselves, "A bad wind is blowing our way." It was as if the devil himself had come for a visit and decided to stay. The peace that Woodloe Plantation once knew came to a bitter end.

It all began to happen the first Sunday morning that Isaac was there. This Sunday morning, when normally the field slaves were allowed to take time off to rest and be with their families, Isaac woke them up with a big cowbell. It was a cowbell usually used in case of a fire, so all the slaves came running. But there was no fire, at least not one they could see. The fire was inside Isaac. A fire fueled by hate. They were all told to get dressed, go to the fields, and put in a full day's work.

Old Jordan stepped forward, with eyes looking at the ground in front of him, and said, "Sir, we's never works a full day on Sunday, unless we's did something wrong."

However, before the words could get all the way out of Old Jordan's mouth, Isaac walked over to him and struck his face with the butt of a whip. With this one blow, he knocked out three of Old Jordan's teeth. Everyone froze as Old Jordan just lay on the ground bleeding.

"You niggers do what I tell you, and when I tell you, and you never talk back to me. Now get," Isaac said as he turned and walked back towards the big house. That should put the fear of God in them, he thought as he smiled to himself.

Robert helped Old Jordan stand up and brushed him off. He picked up the teeth off the ground and put them in his pocket.

"I'll see what Master Jones has to say about this," Robert told Old Jordan as they walked towards Old Jordan's house. I know Lew doesn't know what's going on, he thought.

The slaves went off to the fields and began to work. They talked amongst themselves in low voices because they were afraid. Most of them had never seen anyone get hit the way they had just witnessed. Master Jones never hit anyone, so they wondered why he would allow this. After all, he was the Master, not Isaac. Besides, Isaac wasn't even his son. He was an outsider. This was Master Jones' plantation, and they were Master Jones' slaves, not Isaac's.

Lew was awakened by the smell of Ada's biscuits. She made biscuits every Sunday morning, and the smell of them cooking would work its way all through the house like a thief trying to steal those last few minutes of sleep one had left in the morning. Lew had not heard the cowbell, and did not know what had happened outside. He walked over to his bedroom window wiping the sleep from his eyes. To his surprise he saw the slaves in the fields working. Lew knew today was Sunday. Ada's biscuits told him that. He thought to himself, did someone do something wrong, and why hadn't his father told him about it?

Lew got dressed and went downstairs to the breakfast room.

"Good morning Master Lew," said Ada as he entered the room.

"Morning Ada," he said, and then he spoke to his mother, father, and Isaac. As he sat down, he said, "Father, what is going on with the slaves in the fields today?"

His father looked at him with his hazel eyes, and then looked at Mrs. Jones.

"It's your brother's idea. He's going to run the plantation for a while. Besides, we hear that war is coming and things have to change on the plantation. We need to stock up on everything and accumulate all the money we can get. Things might get rough."

Lew couldn't believe what he was hearing, and didn't like it one bit. He let everyone know it without saying a single word. They knew just by the look on his face. It was the way his greenish-blue eyes came close together, almost closing. He stood up and just walked out of the room.

Lew left the house and went out into the cane field.

"Robert," he shouted. "Come here."

"Yes Lew," Robert replied as he walked over to where Lew was kicking a lump of hard clay. He noticed the look on Lew's face and asked, "What's wrong?"

Lew told him what his father had said about Isaac running the plantation, and war coming. Robert didn't understand this thing about war coming. He asked Lew why Isaac had hit Old Jordan so hard that he knocked out his teeth just for asking a question. Robert then opened his hand and showed Lew the three teeth. Once they had been pearly white but now they were covered with blood. Lew was stunned.

"He beat old Jordan?" he asked.

"Yes," Robert replied.

"Damn him, damn him to hell, I'm not going to allow this, brother or no brother."

Lew quickly started back to the big house. Suddenly, Lew stopped and turned, "Give me those teeth," he said. "Give me those damn teeth."

When Lew returned to the house he heard the sound of laughter coming from the breakfast room. The sounds could be heard all through the house. As he walked, he noticed that the house slaves all appeared to be afraid and unhappy, especially Ada and Enoch. Lew walked to the table where Isaac was sitting and stood over him. He looked him in his eyes, those same cold blue eyes that everyone feared, and asked, "You hit Old Jordan because he asked you a question?"

"No," Isaac said as he looked at his mother and smiled.

"Who would tell you a thing like that, Old Jordan?"

"No," Lew said, "Robert told me."

"Robert," Isaac replied, "I knew that nigger was going to be trouble, and he's a liar." With this Isaac got up from the table. "Excuse me," he said, and kissed his mother on his way out of the room. "A slave lying on a white man, we'll see about this," he said as he walked out of the house.

Mrs. Jones said in her weak high pitched voice, "That uppity nigger Robert, that uppity lying nigger done lied on my son."

Lew looked at her, then walked over to his father and placed the teeth that he had been holding in his hand on the table in front of him.

"Well I guess that Old Jordan knocked out his own teeth," he said, and walked out of the door behind Isaac.

Lew didn't notice the blood coming from his hand. He didn't realize that he had become so angry that he had squeezed the teeth until they cut the skin in the palm of his hand. He didn't have time to think about that now. He was thinking about the look in Ada's eyes as she stood there listening to Mrs. Jones talk about Robert. Lew had looked at her big brown eyes and seen the sadness in them.

"What have I done," he asked himself. "I have forgotten my first school lesson. 'Be known by silence.'" Then he began to run towards the cane field.

"Come here nigger, come here you nigger called Robert," Isaac yelled at the top of his voice. "Nigger get your no count self over here."

Robert ran over to where Isaac was standing. He saw Lew coming and looked at him. Lew looked back at Robert, then they both looked at Isaac.

"Yes Sir Master Isaac," Robert said looking at the ground in front of him. Robert didn't dare look in his eyes. Those hateful blue eyes. For the first time in his life he was afraid. Afraid of Isaac, and what he might do to him.

"Did you tell Lew I beat that nigger Jordan?" Isaac asked him with his face only inches away from Robert's face.

Robert could smell his breath. He could smell the biscuits that his mother had baked on Isaac's breath. His legs began to shake and he said in a low voice, "I said you hit Old Jordan, yes sir."

"I didn't beat anybody, are you calling me a liar boy?!" Isaac yelled.

Robert took a step back, looked at Lew, and then at the ground. They both knew what Isaac was doing. They both knew that no slave would ever call a white man a liar. So they both knew what Robert had to say.

"No sir Master Isaac, you didn't beat Old Jordan sir."

"You lying nigger, get back to work," Isaac said. As he turned and walked away, Lew and Robert heard him say in a low voice, "I'll fix that uppity nigger."

"I'm so sorry Robert," Lew said. "I didn't mean to get you in trouble."

They both knew that Isaac wasn't going to let this go. He wasn't going to let Robert get away with telling on him. They both knew that Isaac would do something, but what? Lew walked over to where Old Jordan was.

"You okay Jordan?" he asked.

He could see the pain in Old Jordan's eyes, and the blood rolling down his face. His face was swollen where the whip had knocked out his teeth.

"Go wash your face and stay in your house for the rest of the day," Lew told him.

Old Jordan looked at Lew's hand and saw the blood dripping down his fingers.

"You bleedin Master Lew. Come let me clean that up for you."

Old Jordan and Lew went to Old Jordan's house. Once there, Jordan got a pot of water off the stove, and a rag from a box at the foot of his bed, an old bed that he had been allowed to keep when it was thrown out of the big house. He washed the blood from Lew's hand and then reached up in a corner of the room. He caught part of a spider's web and put it on Lew's cuts.

"This should stop the bleedin," Old Jordan said.

With that, Lew turned and walked out the door. "Thanks," he said, and closed the door behind him.

As Lew walked back to the big house he knew he had to do something about his brother, but what? How do you deal with a brother that you don't know, and one you don't like. Isaac had been on Woodloe for less than a week, and had caused all kinds of trouble. His mind raced as he walked slowly back to the big house.

When he got to the house, he went to the kitchen. Ada was washing dishes and had seen and heard everything. By the look in her eyes, Lew knew she was afraid for her son, afraid of what Isaac would do to him. She knew that Mrs. Jones did not like Robert. Now, Isaac was out to get him. Ada began to cry. She covered her mouth with her apron so no one in the house could hear her. Lew couldn't take it anymore. He had never seen Ada cry in all the years that he had known her. Lew had never seen the look he saw that day in those big brown eyes. He knew what he had to do.

Lew walked out of the kitchen and into the breakfast room. He walked up to Isaac, looked him straight in his eyes, and said, "don't you ever lay a hand on Old Jordan or Robert again. If you do, brother or not, you will have to deal with me."

Master Jones and his wife just sat there with their mouths wide opened. They looked as if they wanted to say something but couldn't speak. They were shocked, but at the same time they knew that Lew meant what he had said and so did Isaac.

As Lew walked out of the room, Isaac said, "Well sir, the boy does have a backbone."

Hearing this, Lew stopped, turned and looked at Isaac once more but didn't say anything. He turned back around and walked out of the house.

CHAPTER 5

▼

In the weeks that followed, conditions on Woodloe Plantation only got worst for the slaves. The talk was that people from the northern states said all the slaves would soon be free. The slaves at Woodloe didn't know what being free meant, or even where free was. Until Isaac came to the plantation and started all this trouble, most of the time they were happy. Isaac, fearing that the slaves would get in their minds to free themselves, started beating somebody every day to keep them afraid and unsure about whatever was going on. Whoever he beat didn't have to do anything; Isaac just had to beat someone. Nevertheless, he didn't touch Old Jordan or Robert. He hardly even said a word to either of them. No, he had other plans for them. But, he beat everyone else, gave them no days off, and cut back on the food they were given. It didn't matter who Isaac beat, man, woman, or child. He seemed to enjoy mistreating people.

About six months later, Enoch was in the house cleaning and polishing furniture when he overheard Isaac talking to Master Jones.

"I told you that I would make more money for you. Take a look at the books. We have nearly doubled our profits in the last six months. We both know that the war is coming and we will be ready for it, and we don't have to worry about any of those niggers trying anything. For I have put the fear of God in every one of them niggers. They know who runs this place, and they know not to even think about trying anything. We have stocked up on everything and we have plenty of money. Sir, you know when this war starts we are going to need it."

Master Jones knew that he didn't need the money that Isaac had made for him. Before Isaac came, the plantation was doing fine. He was already rich, as was his father before him.

Enoch had heard talk about money before and knew it was something powerful because he'd seen some slaves who had actually bought themselves and lived without masters. He was pretty sure that's what freedom was. But for himself he had always enjoyed his work in the big house, even though he often worked seven days a week and sometimes from dawn until past midnight. Part of his duties was to be on hand when Master Jones woke up and to be there when he went to bed, doing whatever he commanded, just like Ada did whatever Mrs. Jones commanded. He had never thought about the possibility of buying himself or living free until he heard Isaac talk so much about money and everything they could do with it.

Like everybody else at Woodloe, Enoch knew why Master Jones let Isaac do the things he did. He let him have his way to please Mrs. Jones, just to keep her happy. Maybe she felt bad about all of the years that she had spent away from her son Isaac. Now she could make up for all that lost time by letting him do whatever he wanted. This made her happy, and Master Jones was willing to keep her happy at any cost. He truly was in love with his wife and for her sake had turned a blind eye to the things Isaac did. But, was he willing to pay the cost of pretending everything was ok when he knew it wasn't?

Enoch was one of the few slaves who still respected Master Jones, mostly because of his own position and the fact of the blood they probably shared somewhere down the line. Far worse, though, than the loss of the slaves' respect for Master Jones was the loss of his son Lew's respect for him. Yes, Lew, his own son had no respect for him now, and was barely saying anything to his mother. In fact, Lew spent most of his time in Ada's house talking to Robert. He promised Robert that he would do something to stop Isaac.

On July 6, 1861, Lew Jones and Robert's seventeenth birthday, Lew convinced his father to let everyone have the day off to celebrate. The big house was decorated with ribbons and banners. Long tables and benches were made and placed in the yard. They were put on the side of the big house, between it and the slaves quarters. The head table was draped with a white tablecloth. There were three vases placed on it. On each side of the head table were three other tables. The tables were filled with foods of all kinds; cakes, pies, chicken, wild turkey, fish, crabs, greens, potato salad, you name it, and it was there.

Ada and two other slaves cooked for two days to prepare for the event. The men killed a hog and cooked it over an open fire. Old Jordan was the best cook on the plantation when it came to barbeque, and everyone knew it. He stood over the hog, mopping it with a mixture of seasonings, vinegar, a little cane sugar, and bacon grease. The meat was golden brown and calling out to be eaten. The aroma floated across the plantation and filled the air from the stone arch of the front gate to the muddy banks of the Moon River. One could smell it for miles around as it cooked slowly. Old Jordan had been cooking it since before sunrise that morning.

A few of the slaves stood around the pit with Old Jordan, laughing and joking. They seemed to be having the time of their lives. Some of them played mouth harps, fiddles, hambones, and spoons. The sound of music filled the air as people danced. This was a good day to be on Woodloe Plantation and the first time in a long time that everyone enjoyed themselves without being afraid. At about twelve o'clock noon, Master Jones came out of the big house with Mrs. Jones holding onto his right arm. They walked over to the center table and sat down. "Let's eat," he shouted, and all the slaves cheered.

Lew and Robert were in the field of wildflowers when they heard Master Jones call. They had been reflecting on the fact that this was the first day that everybody on the plantation seemed happy since Isaac had come there. At the sound of Master Jones' voice they both jumped up and started running toward the big house.

"Boy, you gittin to be an old man," Robert told Lew.

"Just like you," Lew replied as they smiled and raced to the tables. Lew ran over to the head table and sat down next to his father. Robert sat at the table with Old Jordan.

"Where is Isaac?" Mrs. Jones asked.

At about that time, Isaac walked out of the side door of the house. He was dressed in the same black outfit he had worn on the day he arrived at Woodloe. Everyone got quiet as he walked to the head table with a package in his hand. He walked up behind Lew and placed the package on the table in front of him. It was a box about twelve inches long and four inches thick.

"Happy birthday," said Isaac, waiting for Lew to open the box. "Well go on, it's not going to bite you."

Isaac sat down next to his mother. Lew opened the box. Inside were two Colt 44 revolvers with pearl handles.

"You're a man now, and every man should own a gun," Isaac said with a smile on his face.

"Thank you," said Lew as he closed the lid of the box. He then looked at Robert and the other slaves who were all staring at him silently. Lew didn't like guns and most of them knew it. He never had any use for them and never wanted to.

"Bring on the pig," shouted Master Jones.

Old Jordan cut off a ham, and placed in on the head table. He then began cutting the other parts and placing them on the other tables.

"Boy that's pretty," Master Jones said, and they all began to eat.

This was a day they would remember for years to come. Master Lew's seventeenth birthday, the biggest party that Woodloe Plantation had seen in a while. Around one o'clock, Ada walked out of the big house with a cake. There were seventeen candles burning brightly on it. She put it on the table in front of Lew, and everyone started singing and clapping their hands. Lew sat there with his greenish-blue eyes shining, and a big smile on his face. He cut a piece for everyone at the head table, then he told Ada to cut pieces for everyone else.

An hour later, Master Jones and his wife went back into the big house. Lew and Isaac remained at the head table, watching the slaves dancing and enjoying themselves.

"Just look at them," Isaac said. "They are just like little children, dancing around and acting like fools. They better enjoy this day because tomorrow I'm going to make them make it up."

Lew turned and looked at Isaac. Without saying a word he then got up and walked away. He left the guns Isaac gave him on the table but would find them on his bed later that night. Looking around for Robert, Lew didn't see him. After eating so much food, Robert could hardly move and had gone home to take a nap. As he lay on his pallet rubbing his stomach, he heard someone walking towards the house. They stopped at the front door and knocked.

"Who is it?" Robert asked.

"Me."

Robert recognized Lew's voice. He got up and opened the door.

"Boy, you know that you never knocked on the door before. Why didn't you just come in?"

"Because I knew you were in that bed and I wanted to make you get up."

They smiled. Then Lew handed Robert a package wrapped in the prettiest paper he had ever seen.

"What's this?"

"It's your birthday too," said Lew. "Happy birthday."

Robert slowly unwrapped the paper. He didn't want to tear it. Inside, he found a bible.

"Thank you. Thank you very much."

Lew gave him a big hug, then walked out of the door. Robert sat on his bed and stared at the bible. It was the first book that he had ever owned. In fact, none of the other slaves on the plantation owned any books. None of them could read. If they could, he didn't know about it. Then again, none of them knew that he could read. Robert put the bible on a shelf next to his bed, and went to sleep.

CHAPTER 6

▼

It was dark when Robert woke up. The party was over and Ada was just coming home.

"Hi mama," Robert said as Ada walked in the door. "Let me go get you some water to wash your clothes."

He grabbed the empty pots from the top of the stove, and headed out the door. When he returned, Ada was sitting on a wooden chair holding the bible.

"What is this book?" she asked.

"It's my birthday present. Lew gave it to me," Robert said smiling.

"Boy, have you two fools lost your minds?" Ada shouted. Then she lowered her voice and said, "We can't have no books boy. Besides, you can't read a word in it."

"But I can mama," Robert said as he took the book from her hand. He opened it and began to read, "In the beginning, God created the heavens and the earth."

"Hush up boy," Ada said in a low voice. "Hide that bible and don't you ever let anyone know that you can read, never. Do you hear me son?"

Robert just looked at his mother and closed the bible. He then placed it in a box at the foot of his bed, under some clothes. Ada didn't say anything else that night. She washed her clothes, got into her bed and went to sleep. She was proud that Robert could read, but at the same time she was afraid for him. She knew that slaves weren't supposed to learn.

The next morning when Robert woke up, Ada had already gone to the big house. He saw a package wrapped in brown paper on the table. He knew it was a present from his mother. She had forgotten to give it to him the night before. He picked it up, unwrapped the paper and found a pretty red handkerchief. He smiled and wrapped it around his neck.

Robert heard the other slaves walking around outside. He dressed and went outside. As he walked, he looked at the tables that were still in the yard and smiled. He then headed for the rice fields. When Robert arrived, Old Jordan was already working at the edge of a field. He looked at him and said, "You a might pretty sight this morning with that thing around your neck, and you sleepin a mite late aren't you?" They both smiled. Then Robert began to work, using a metal hoe to dig a long groove in the ground to help prevent over flooding in the field during the hard summer rains.

Isaac proved that he meant what he had told Lew on his birthday. He made life a living hell for the slaves throughout the entire day. None of them got a minute's rest. He made them work until long after the sun went down. He might have lost control for one day but he had it back now.

About two days later, the slaves were in the fields working when they heard a loud noise coming from the road. Riders, about ten men on horseback raced towards the big house. Clouds of dust rose from their horses and covered them from head to toe as they hurried towards the house. Isaac was in the field and ran towards the house when he saw the men. Enoch had been sweeping off the front porch when he looked up and saw the riders. He stepped back inside the house and yelled, "Master Jones, come quick. A whole bunch'a men coming on horseback."

One of the men jumped off his horse and ran to the front door.

"Where is your master?!" he shouted at Enoch.

Master Jones came running down the steps with Lew and Mrs. Jones behind him. They recognized the excited man as Thomas Mitchell, one of their neighbors from eight miles down the road.

"It's war!" Thomas shouted, "We are at war!"

Master Jones, Lew, and Isaac stood there without saying anything for a moment because they didn't know what to say. Then Thomas added, "If I was you, I would lock those niggers up somewhere, and lock them up now! You remember what happened with that Nat Turner nigger don't you?" He then turned around, walked off the porch and got back on his horse. "Lock them up," he said to the group as he rode off.

"We've got to do it," said Isaac. "We got to do it right now! We got to get them niggers out of the fields and lock them up somewhere so that we can check them for weapons. We've got to take anything that they could use as a weapon. We've got to get the cane knives, the hoes, anything and everything they've got."

Master Jones and Lew just stood there looking at Isaac. They didn't know what to make of all this. They both knew the slaves on the plantation, and trusted them. Then Lew looked at his father and said, "If you hadn't let Isaac treat them the way he did, you wouldn't have anything to worry about."

His father looked into Lew's green-blue eyes and didn't say a word, he couldn't, for Lew had told the truth.

"Damn that," said Isaac, "I'm getting my guns and I'll kill the first one that looks at me the wrong way." He then ran back up the stairs.

Master Jones walked out onto the front lawn. He had to do something, but what? Mrs. Jones came out of the house and walked over to where Master Jones was standing.

"I'm afraid," said Mrs. Jones, with tears streaming down her face. "I'm a might afraid."

She put her arms around her husband's waist and cried. Master Jones took her by the hand and walked back into the house. He told Lew to round all the slaves up.

"Tell them to all come to the front lawn, right now. The house slaves too, all of them."

At that very moment, Isaac came down the staircase. He had his whip in his hand and a gun holster around his waist. He had two pearl handled colt 45's that looked just like the ones he had given Lew. The guns gleamed as the light bounced off of them.

"Mother you have nothing to be afraid of, not as long as I'm around," he said, leaving the house and walking towards the front lawn. He got the larger cowbell and began to ring it. It was the same one he rang when he first took away their Sundays off the day he hit Old Jordan and called Robert a liar.

Slowly, all the slaves came from the fields, the sheds, and the house where they had been working. One by one they came and stood silently in front of the big house. Not one of them said a word. The house slaves walked out the side door and around the house, then slowly joined the crowd. When all the slaves had gathered together, Master Jones told Lew to count them. Lew did as he was told and shouted out "Ninety-three." Then Master Jones began to talk.

"I've known most of you for all of your lives, and some of you have known me all of my life. What I'm about to say and do is one of the hardest things I've ever had to do." Then he said, as they gazed into his sad hazel eyes, "I guess that you have all heard that we are at war with the North." He stopped, then took a deep breath, and continued. "I don't know what kind of ideas those northerners are trying to put in your heads, but I tell you now, it's not going to work. Not on

Woodloe Plantation, ever. You are all Jones' slaves. Your were born Jones' slaves and you will die Jones' slaves, and you best remember this."

Then he told all of them to go to their houses and bring him all their house knives, cane knives, spades, axes or hatchets, hoes and saws, anything sharp that could be used as a weapon. The slaves walked away, each to his or her own house. You could hear them talking in low voices as they went along. They were all frightened, more frightened than they had ever been in their lives.

CHAPTER 7

▼

Fear became the order of the day on Woodloe Plantation. Master Jones and his wife were frightened, Isaac was frightened, and all of the slaves were frightened. The only one who was not afraid was Lew. Maybe because of all the books he had read, he seemed to know something that no one else knew.

Meanwhile, the field slaves wanted to know what the men who had rode up to the big house had told Master Jones. They did not stop passing messages and questions to Enoch and Ada and the other house slave until they found out why Master Jones was so upset and acting the way he was. He thought that his slaves would turn on him and his family like Nat Turner. He also knew that if he had not let Isaac mistreat them the way that he had, he wouldn't be worried half as much as he was. Still, he thought he had to protect his family. He had to do what he was doing.

One by one the slaves brought knives, shovels, and anything else that they thought Master Jones believed could be used as a weapon. They placed these items on the ground near the spot where the Master stood and backed away from them. They just stood there with their eyes fixed on the Master, perfectly silent, waiting for the others to come one by one with their knives and tools. When they all had brought the so-called weapons, they were told to just stand where they were. Then Master Jones walked with Lew and Isaac into the big house. He told them to search the slave quarters one by one.

"Don't miss anything, search every nook and cranny," he said.

Lew hurried to Ada's cabin. He remembered he had given Robert that bible for his birthday. He couldn't take any chances on Isaac finding it. Lew walked into the house and looked around. He sat on Ada's bed, the bed that he had slept in as an infant and toddler, and where he used to lay talking to his best friend in the world. Why, he asked himself, why was all this happening, and what could he do about it? He had to do something with all this talk about slaves killing people and all, but what? Lew got up, slowly walked out of the cabin, and on to the next one.

At the same time, Isaac was busy tearing up the cabins that he searched. He threw things around and broke up the little possessions that the slaves had. He had a real look of fear in his face as those cold blue eyes darted from corner to another in every cabin he entered. As he walked into each, he remembered how he had beat and mistreated the slaves that lived there. He remembered how he enjoyed mistreating them, and now he was afraid. For the first time since he had set foot on Woodloe Plantation, he was actually afraid. He had thought to himself that he would kill every single slave before he let them know that he was afraid of them. He rubbed the two guns that rode on his hips and mumbled in a low voice, "every damn last one of them."

It took most of the day for Lew and Isaac to finish searching the slave quarters. When they had, Master Jones told the slaves to return to their homes. The house slaves were told not to return to the big house unless someone came to get them. Master Jones told Ada to go back into the house to cook that night's supper. As she walked towards the side of the house, Ada looked in the faces of the other slaves. Fear, despair, and anger were in their eyes, the same eyes that at one time had only reflected peace and happiness living on Woodloe Plantation. But all that seemed like a hundred years ago now.

Ada opened the kitchen screen door only to find Mrs. Jones standing there. She held a long kitchen knife and shook as if it was the coldest day in winter, but this was April and the weather was warm.

"Don't you come in my house," Mrs. Jones shouted, "You niggers ain't killing me. I don't trust none of you, so you get out right now."

For the first time in years, Ada looked into Mrs. Jones eyes. She looked deep into those hate-filled blue eyes of Mrs. Jones, then dropped her head without saying a word. She turned and walked out of the house.

As she reached the front of the house near the area where Master Jones, Lew and Isaac stood, she stopped and looked at Master Jones. When he saw her there, he asked why she wasn't in the kitchen making supper.

Ada replied, "Mrs. Jones run me out with a knife, talking about I ain't killin her. Sir, I just went there cause you told me to cook supper. I ain't thinking about killin nobody."

Master Jones just shook his head as he told Ada to go home then walked towards the kitchen. It was then that he heard Mrs. Jones screaming. Master Jones hurried inside the house and found his wife shaking with the knife still in her hand. He walked over to her and slowly took the knife from her hand, then he hugged her. Lew and Isaac followed Master Jones into the house and saw the state that their mother was in. Then Isaac said as he looked into his mother's eyes, "Them niggers, they the cause of this. That Ada must have done something to mother when she came in here. She was all alone with mother, and she did something to her."

Master Jones and Lew looked at each other and smiled. For they both knew Ada, and they both knew that Ada would never hurt anyone or anything.

"I'll find out what it was, even if I have to beat the black off of her. I'll find out what she did to my mother," said Isaac.

As he turned towards the door, Master Jones grabbed his arm.

"You won't lay one finger on Ada," he said. "Now help Lew get your mother upstairs. I have to get dinner started."

The two boys took their mother up to her room, and helped her prepare for bed. She asked Isaac to stay with her for a while, because she didn't want to be alone. Lew left them and went back to the kitchen to help his father cook. He had spent hours watching Ada cook, and he had learned a lot from her. He knew that his father couldn't boil water without hurting someone, so he told his father that he would cook supper. However, Master Jones insisted that he do the cooking, so Lew let him.

Meanwhile, Mrs. Jones and Isaac were upstairs in her bedroom. Mrs. Jones pointed out how her husband had just protected Ada, and how he was always bragging about Robert.

"Them two niggers got some kind of voodoo on him or something," Isaac told her. "The way he carry on over them isn't natural."

"Son, I don't care what you have to do," Mrs. Jones said. "Make them niggers pay, make them pay for all of this."

"Yes mama," Isaac said, "I will."

Then he left her room and went to his.

CHAPTER 8

▼

As the night came, you could feel the tension in the big house grow. It spread through every room like the foul smell of something rotten. Mrs. Jones barely ate anything and kept complaining about not being able to close her eyes, afraid to go to sleep. Isaac kept walking from room to room, window to window, looking for anything that moved in the darkness. Master Jones stayed in the sitting room having a drink of whiskey made from the cane syrup he grew on his plantation. Lew finished the book he was reading and went to sleep. The night went on pretty much this way until dawn, when Isaac shouted, "Someone is riding up the road headed for the house."

Master Jones got up from his high back chair and pulled down a rifle from over the fireplace. The noise woke Lew up and he looked in his mother's room before going down the stairs. They all walked outside onto the front porch, Master Jones holding his rifle, and Isaac with both his guns in his hands. Lew stood behind the two of them waiting to see what would happen. As the lone rider got closer, they saw that he was a white man dressed in a gray uniform, black boots, and a sword on his side.

"What do you want," shouted Master Jones.

"Morning," he said, "I'm Captain Bogart Davis, and I'm recruiting men to fight this war. All I need is a few good men. I guess I don't have to tell you what is at stake here, our homes, our lives, our very existence. Those bastards from the North are trying to take it all away from us. We need good men, every man that is willing to stand up for this way of life that we have come to know and love. The way of life our fathers, and their fathers knew. We can not, and we will not let outsiders come down here and tell us how to live our lives. Not now, not ever."

The fire in his voice filled the morning air, and touched something deep down inside of Master Jones and Isaac. Lew, on the other hand, was not impressed by this speech. It sounded as if the captain had said it over and over every place he had been, and now it was the people at Woodloe's turn to hear it. The uniform and the sword, however, did impress Isaac.

"When do you need us sir," Isaac said standing straight, as if he were already a soldier.

"The sooner the better," said Captain Davis. "Report to the recruiting station on River Street, and we will sign you up. How about you son," he said, looking at Lew.

Lew turned, looked into his father's eyes, then said, "There are some things that need attending to on the plantation first, then maybe I'll think about join-ing. First, I have things to see about around here."

"Good enough," said Captain Davis, then he got back on his horse and rode away.

Lew knew that he would never join any army. He didn't feel as though the war had anything to do with him or Woodloe Plantation. He knew it had some-thing to do with slavery, and with slaves becoming free. Still, at the same time, he knew that it was about more than that. The whole thing was about money. Yes, money. It was about the money that the white people in the South were making off of free slave labor.

Lew had also seen the way many people treated their slaves. He saw his sick minded half brother kick, whip, and mistreat the slaves right there on Woodloe Plantation. And for what? Just to say that he made more money. Money that his father could have done without. Now, because of this, it looked as if their whole world was coming apart all around them. In one way or another, they were all afraid of what Isaac had created. He had taken a once peaceful plantation and sin-gle handedly turned it into a place where Mr. and Mrs. Jones were afraid for their very lives. Isaac was afraid for his life because of the dirt he had done. However, Lew was not afraid for his life but for the lives of the slaves on the plantation. He feared that harm would come to them and they would be killed for no reason except being slaves.

Lew had to see about Robert, Ada, and the rest of the slaves. He knew that the plantation would be in severe shape if he left it in its present state with everyone afraid, master and slave both locked in their houses. Lew knew that he could only make things better after Isaac was gone. He was glad Isaac had told the captain that he would join his army and looked forward to the day he would see Isaac leave.

CHAPTER 9

▼

The plantation was already suffering from the effects of this war. Hardly a week had passed since the slaves were told to go in their houses and stay. Already, things on the plantation were falling apart. The animals, the fields, and lawns, everything needed tending to. Worst of all was inside the big house. Without Ada or Enoch to keep the place organized and clean, it had become a mess.

Master Jones did all the cooking himself, though he didn't know how to do it well. And the fact was, Mrs. Jones could have cooked and cleaned but she wouldn't. She wouldn't even come down the stairs, something she hadn't done since Isaac and Lew helped put her to bed. Little did anyone know at that time that she would never come down the steps again, at least not on her own. Fear had a hold on her, a fear that was strong and powerful, and wouldn't let go. That same fear made her walk from room to room, looking out of every window on the top floor of the house. Her son did the same thing downstairs at night. With her cold blue eyes darting back and forth, Mrs. Jones watched everything that moved. She spent endless hours of the day and night watching, until she could take no more and had to sleep. When she woke up she would start all over again, walking from room to room. Then she stopped eating, and stopped doing anything but watching and waiting. She was waiting on what she called them "uppity niggers." The ones she hated. The ones that were out to get her.

Mrs. Jones' behavior caused Master Jones to worry about his wife. Because she would not eat, she became more frail by the day. He worried about his plantation, his slaves, and about Ada and Robert. Five days came and went, and Master Jones decided that the slaves had to come out of their quarters. They had to do the work. However, no one was to come near the big house for any reason. Master Jones told them that they would be shot if they did. The house slaves were told that they were now field slaves. This made them angry, especially when the field slaves laughed at them. For house slaves always thought that they were better than field slaves. This was just the way it had always been.

The slaves had to work with their bare hands or wooden tools without any metal attached, which made their work go very slowly. The cane had to be pulled up by hand. The dirt had to be turned with wooden shovels. The grass had to be torn instead of cut. Whatever had to be done had to be done without metal tools, for they could and might be used as weapons.

Ada was told to come back into the kitchen. She would be the only slave allowed to return to the big house. Prompted by fear, Isaac took all but one knife out of the kitchen. He didn't notice, but it was the same one his mother had been holding when she threatened Ada. He put the rest of the knives in a cabinet in the dinning room and locked it. Ada was instructed not to go in any other room of the house besides the kitchen.

Mrs. Jones wouldn't like Ada being back in the house, but Master Jones couldn't take trying to cook anymore. For some reason, he didn't want Lew to do the cooking either. He said that it had to be done. Ada had to come back in the house to cook. When it was time for Ada to come and go, Master Jones would tell Lew to go upstairs and talk with Mrs. Jones. Lew would get her away from the windows. Only then could Master Jones sneak Ada in and out.

Lew liked having Ada back in the house. He had missed her being around. He also missed talking with her. As soon as she got inside the house, Lew came down the stairs and headed for the kitchen. He got a stool and sat it next to the big table where Ada was making bread. He just sat there at first, not saying a word. Then he hopped off of the stool and gave Ada a big hug.

"Mama Ada," he said, "I'm so sorry about all this mess, and I'm sorry for the way that all of you have been mistreated."

He asked her about Robert. He hadn't seen him in about five days. This was the first time that the two of them had been away from each other for so long.

"He's angry," replied Ada. "He's angry that Master could ever think that we would ever try to hurt him, or anyone else on the plantation. Well, maybe Isaac, but that's another story."

They both laughed.

"Well, nobody could blame him," Lew answered, "but let's not talk about that."

Little did they know that Isaac was standing in the hallway outside of the kitchen door. He was listening and had heard every word the two of them had said.

"That nigger Robert. I knew he was up to no good. He wants to kill me," Isaac said to himself. "I'll show him. I'll show him good."

Isaac got his whip and walked out of the front door of the house. He headed for the cane fields where Robert was working. He had his guns at his sides, and the whip in his hand. The end of the whip dragged the ground behind him as he walked. His cold blue eyes searched all over for the spot where Robert was working. Then he saw him, but Robert didn't see Isaac coming. Robert was bent down and pulling cane when he felt a pain that he had never in his life felt before. It was the sting of Isaac's whip on his back. Robert fell down to his knees from the pain, and looked up at Isaac. He could see the hate that filled his eyes.

"Master Isaac!" he shouted, "What did I do?"

Still the whip didn't stop, and Robert got no answer. He was hit again and again, over and over. The whip tore the skin from his flesh until Roberts's eyes rolled back in his head. He couldn't cry out in pain anymore, and he passed out. Only then did the whipping stop. Isaac stood over Robert; breathing hard and looking down at him, smiling at Robert's motionless body down in the dirt. Blood covered the ground all around him.

Isaac, with the smile still on his face, said, "This will teach you to threaten me. You thought I had forgotten about the time you lied on me, but I knew that I would get you sooner or later. You not so uppity now, are you? You uppity nigger."

The slaves that had been working nearby stopped what they were doing. They stood there with their eyes fixed on the spot where Robert laid covered with blood. Some of them became ill, and the children began to cry. They had seen Isaac beat slaves before, but never like this, never this viciously. Tears fell from Old Jordan's wise and aged brown eyes. He cried for Robert laying in the dirt in pain, barely able to move.

Isaac looked around at them all, and said, "let this be a lesson to all of you. I'll kill any of you who even think about killing me."

What he didn't know was that Robert had never thought about hurting him or anyone else. Isaac kicked some dirt in Robert's face, then turned and walked back towards the big house. He left behind him Robert's blood, dripping from his whip as he walked away. As Isaac neared the house, he washed his whip in the water trough near the front porch. Then he went into the house and up the stairs.

He had to tell his mother what he had overheard from Ada and Lew, and what he had done about it.

As Isaac described the way he had beat Robert, his mother's eyes lit up. It was as if she herself had delivered every painful blow of the whip. Then she smiled and said, "Good, that little uppity nigger got what he had coming to him."

Isaac told his mother that he had done it for her. She said she was proud of him and thanked him. He didn't say a word about the beating to Master Jones or Lew. He knew that they would find out soon enough. Besides, Robert had had it coming. He was a troublemaker, and the other slaves looked to him as if he was some kind of leader or something. The fact was that Isaac had heard the words come from Lew's own mouth that Robert was thinking about hurting him. No matter what happened, Lew couldn't deny it.

Out in the cane field, several slaves picked Robert's bleeding body up off the ground. They carried him down to the river, and put him in the salt water. Robert became conscious and let out a scream so terrible that it scared everyone around him, then he passed out again from the pain. Old Jordan started removing the torn bloody clothes that Robert wore, the small bloody pieces of rags that had once been his shirt and pants. They were the same clothes Master Jones had given him when they went into town together.

Some of the slaves went to their houses and got clean rags. Old Jordan told one of them to bring him some ashes from the burned cocker burrows of the pine tree. This would help to heal the cuts after the salt water helped stop some of the bleeding. Some of the cuts were so deep that a mixture of ashes and red clay had to be packed into the deeply opened flesh wounds. They then placed Robert on a board, and two of the men began to carry him home. The other slaves went back to work for fear that Isaac would come out of the house and do the same to them. They didn't know what Robert had done. All they knew was that he had been working right along with them when it happened.

Old Jordan stood by the river for a few moments, then followed behind the men carrying Robert. His wise old brown eyes were filled with tears, as he feared for Robert's life. He knew that Robert was going to have to fight for his very life. Old Jordan knew that a fever would set in, and the cuts would continue to bleed, not healing anytime soon. He also knew about the pain that Robert would have to endure day after day. So he cried for the boy who had become like a son to him.

The men put Robert in his mother's bed instead of his own pallet on the floor. Old Jordan stood in front of Ada's cabin, looking over at the big house and hoping she would see him. He wanted to go and tell her what had happened, but remembered Master Jones' words, "Don't come near the house or you will be shot." He turned, went inside Ada's house and closed the door behind him.

Old Jordan asked the men to bring him some fresh water in the pots that were on the stove, the same pots that Robert would fill every day for his mother to wash her clothes. Then he pulled a chair next to the bed, and sat there waiting for Robert to wake up. He told the men that had helped him to go back to work because they might be missed by Isaac. Old Jordan knew there was nothing they could do for Robert now. It was now up to Robert whether he lived or died.

The sun slowly went down and darkness began to fill the room. Old Jordan had fallen asleep. When he awoke, he felt as if death was trying to come into the house. He saw shadows all around him. He jumped up from the chair and lit a candle. He started a fire in the stove then sat back down next to Robert. Robert's body was motionless, so Old Jordan checked his heartbeat to see if he was still alive. He was. Old Jordan put some more cold water on his forehead with the rags. This would keep Robert cool and help break the fever.

CHAPTER 10

▼

As suppertime came in the big house, it appeared as if hearing the news about Robert being beaten brought back Mrs. Jones' appetite. She asked Isaac to go downstairs and bring her something to eat with a glass of sweet tea. After she ate the food, she felt good. In fact, she felt like going downstairs. However, when she went to the head of the staircase, fear took hold of her again, and she returned to her bedroom. As it became darker outside, Mrs. Jones went back to walking from room to room, looking out the windows.

It was long past dark when Ada left the big house. She slowly walked out of the screen door and across the open field. As she got closer to her house, she saw a small group of people standing by her front door.

Ada shouted, "No!" and began to run. The bread in her apron fell to the ground as she ran towards the house. "Robert," she shouted, "no, not my son."

She looked at the sad eyes of the people standing outside of her house. As she went into the house, she saw Old Jordan sitting next to Robert's death-still body. Slowly she inched closer. Her feet barely moved, feeling as if they weighed a hundred pounds each.

"Is he dead?" she asked Old Jordan.

"No, he's not dead, a might close, but he's a fighter."

Ada walked over to the bed. Slowly she looked at her son. His face was so badly swollen and cut that she could hardly recognize him. His body was slashed all over from Isaac's whip. The blood rushed to Ada's head. Her big brown eyes sank back into her head, then she fainted and fell towards the floor. Old Jordan caught her and steered her to the pallet on the floor. My God, he thought to himself, how could a man do this to people that had never hurt anything or anybody in their lives?

The next morning Ada didn't go to the big house. She had become ill from worrying about Robert. The only thing she could think about was him not dying. He was the only child she had. She had already lost the rest of her family. She couldn't bear to lose him too. She stayed in her bed with a fever and tears coming from her eyes. Now Old Jordan had two people that he had to look after, and seeing Ada cry only made him cry too.

Master Jones waited for Ada to show up that morning. When she didn't, he sent Lew to see why. He was ready and waiting for his breakfast, the eggs and ham that Ada cooked just right. Lew ran out the door thinking about his friend Robert. He would finally see him after a week of not talking with him. He looked forward to fooling around with him.

As he got closer to Robert's house, he saw people standing by the front door. He wondered why they weren't in the fields working. Then he knew right away that something was wrong. When he got closer to the door, he heard Ada crying. None of the people outside of the house said a word, for they were also crying. Every one of them had their eyes fixed on the ground, never looking at Lew as he stood by the door.

Once inside, he saw Ada sitting in a chair with her head in her hands crying. He looked at Old Jordan, who was also crying. As he looked at Old Jordan's sad face, he could see that something was terribly wrong. Lew slowly looked next to where Old Jordan was standing. He closed his eyes, rubbed them, and took a second look.

"No," he said, "no, not Robert."

He knew at once who had done this. He knew this was Isaac's handy work. Lew began to cry, as he turned and ran out of the door. He ran towards his house, sweat coming from his forehead, and breathing hard. He ran as fast as he could.

"I'll kill him. I'll kill that no good for nothing half-brother of mine," he said to himself.

He ran in the house and up the stairs. He went to his bedroom and got the guns Isaac had given him for his birthday. Lew quickly put one bullet in one of the guns and proceeded down the steps. With tears coming from his eyes he could hear Isaac's voice. It was coming from the sitting room where Isaac was talking with Master Jones. Lew turned the corner leading into the sitting room and stood in front of the doorway. As tears fell from his greenish-blue eyes, he searched the room for the spot where he heard their voices.

Lew lifted the gun and slowly pointed it at Isaac's head. He had never shot a gun before, but this had to be done. Isaac, who was talking to Master Jones, turned only to see his brother with the gun. He stood still looking around for a place to run. However, Lew was blocking the only way out of the room.

"I told you not to mess with Robert," Lew said, and pulled the trigger.

Isaac fell to the floor as smoke filled the room. Lew stood there, holding the gun, watching and waiting for the smoke to clear. The bullet had missed its mark, Isaac was not hit. As Isaac got up from the floor, Lew remembered that in his haste, he had only put one bullet in the gun.

"I'll kill you," he said, "I'll kill you," as he hit Isaac with the gun, over and over again. Master Jones pulled Lew off Isaac. Master Jones knew the reason Lew was doing this. He also knew that Isaac could no longer stay on Woodloe Plantation. Isaac got up from the floor. His face was bloody and bruised, but not half as bad as Robert's face. Lew stood there breathing hard, ready to jump on him again. The tears had stopped, and Lew asked Isaac why he had done what he had done to Robert. Isaac told Lew how he had overheard Ada and him talking in the kitchen. He reminded Lew what they had said about Robert wanting to hurt him. He also told Lew that he was not going to let Robert get away with thinking that way. Isaac then told Lew that he had to teach Robert, and all of the other slaves a lesson that they would always remember. Now with this he had. He taught every slave on Woodloe Plantation, from Old Jordan the oldest, to little Gladys, the youngest, how to hate him, and he taught them very well. For now, they all hated him.

Master Jones looked at them both and said, "You two are brothers, and shouldn't be acting this way."

Lew looked his father straight in his hazel eyes, and said, "Brother or no, if he stays on this plantation, it will be over my dead body."

Master Jones knew right then and there that Isaac had to leave. He turned and looked at Isaac.

"Isaac," he said, "you were going to join the army. Well, I guess it's time for you to leave."

"I'll be leaving in the morning," Isaac replied. "I'll get my things ready," he added as he walked out of the room.

Isaac went up to his mother's room and found her hiding behind a chair. She had heard the gunshot and fighting. She just knew it was the slaves coming to get her. Isaac told her what had just happened. Then he told her that Master Jones said that it was time for him to leave. The water welled up in her blue eyes and she cried. As Isaac talked Mrs. Jones felt that his having to leave was her fault. She was the one who told him that she disliked Robert. She also knew that Robert had not lied when he said Isaac had hit Old Jordan and knocked out his teeth, but she had kept quiet. She had wanted Robert to pay for all those years she had hated him and his mother, Ada. Still, her happiness hadn't lasted long. For it had caused her two sons to hate each other, and now, her oldest son would have to leave Woodloe Plantation. Mrs. Jones couldn't accept this. She knew what to do.

"I'll talk to Lew. He's my baby and he'll listen to me," she said to herself as Isaac went to his room.

She thought that if Lew saw her crying, he would give in and she could control him. She would make him forgive his brother. After all, Robert was just another slave. So she went to the head of the step and called for Lew. She asked him to come up to her room so that she could speak with him. Lew was talking with his father at the time, and didn't want to go upstairs. He knew Isaac was up there and if he saw him he would beat him again. When Lew reached her bedroom, Mrs. Jones was sitting on her bed with a sad look on her face, her eyes red and swollen from crying.

"Please have a seat next to me," she said. "I heard that you think that your brother did something very bad and—"

Lew stopped her in mid sentence. "I don't have a brother. That man who beat Robert like he did is no human, he's an animal."

Mrs. Jones started crying again, and said, "He's your brother, and my son, please forgive him, please. If he leaves, who will protect me? Who will keep me safe from those niggers."

Lew looked at the water coming from her blue eyes, and for the first time in his life he realized that he didn't know the mother that gave birth to him. The coldness that he had seen in her eyes all those years filled up his heart. He just stood up, and walked out of her room.

"Don't walk away from me," Mrs. Jones cried. "I'm you mother."

Lew turned around slowly and looked her right in her eyes, then said, "Mother? No, you are just the person who gave birth to me. Ada has been more of a mother to me than you have ever been, and Robert has been more of a brother to me than Isaac will ever be."

With that, he walked out of her room, down the steps, and out the front door.

Mrs. Jones came out of her bedroom, threw herself on the floor, and cried. Isaac had been in his bedroom listening the whole time. He came down the hallway and helped his mother back to her room. As he sat on the bed, he said, "This war won't take long. The South is going to win it, and when it's won, I will be back. Then things will be the way they should be, the way that they had been before." He promised her that he would write to her every week, and would return as soon as the war was over. Then he hugged her, and walked out of her room. As he walked down the hallway, he could still hear her crying. Isaac turned around and went back into her room. There, he spent the remainder of that day, and the whole night.

When morning came, Isaac got his bags from his room, kissed his mother on her forehead, then walked down the stairs and out of the house. He didn't say a single word to anyone. He went to the barn, got his horse, and headed for the long road that led off the plantation. On his way down the dirt road, he saw some slaves working. He stopped his horse, and looked down at them. His eyes were filled with hatred as he said, "You niggers best enjoy yourselves now while I'm off fighting this war because I will be back." Then he looked towards the house and rode away.

The slaves stood there and watched as he rode down the road, through the arched gates, and turned left. All at once they began to cheer and dance. He had finally gone. The devil had gone away from Woodloe Plantation. One of the slaves ran to the slave quarters and cane field to tell everyone the good news. All the slaves said that once again there would be peace on the plantation. Little did any of them know at the time that worse things were headed their way. It would come in the form of Confederate soldiers.

Despite Isaac's departure, there was still no peace for Robert, who had to fight for his very life. It had only been a day since he was severely beaten. His pain made it impossible for him to eat or drink anything. He couldn't control his bodily functions and some of the cuts would not stop bleeding. Robert felt like he was in more pain than any one person should have to endure in a lifetime. Most of the time, however, he was unconscious. This was seen as a good thing, because when he was sleeping he couldn't feel the intensity of his pain so deeply. But there was no escaping the pain when he was awake. For Isaac's whip had not only cut into Robert's skin, it had cut into his very soul. It had cut into every good thing that Robert had believed in. Every part of his humanity had been cut away. Now, all that was left was pain.

As Robert lay on his pallet he cried, not only from the pain of the cuts, but from the pain of knowing that he had never done anything to, or against Isaac. All that he had ever said about Isaac was "it didn't matter." That's what he said about most things. He said it about not being able to go into the big house; he said it whenever it came to dealing with white people; and he told himself that it didn't matter whether he lived or died. For he was no longer that hazel-eyed boy with the big smile. That person had been beaten out of him, never to return again. So he cried.

CHAPTER 11

▼

A few days after Isaac left, Sunday came, and all the slaves went to the fields to work. Master Jones woke Lew from his sleep, so that he could go get Ada. He was told to let her in the house while Master Jones kept Mrs. Jones busy. Ada had not been there in three days. Surely she was better by now and could return to work. Today was the day for her to make biscuits, Lew thought as he got out of his bed. He could taste them now, dripping with syrup. As he walked down the hallway past his mother's room, she looked at him. Lew did not want to speak to his mother. He knew that she was partly responsible for Robert's beating. He hadn't spoken a single word to her since he walked out of her room, and didn't care if he never spoke to her again. Master Jones went in to talk with her while Lew went to get Ada. Lew walked out of the kitchen door, and over to Ada's house. He knocked on the door and went in. Ada was sitting next to Robert. Old Jordan stood next to the stove.

"How is he?" Lew asked in a low voice as he looked at Robert.

"Much the same," Old Jordan said walking towards the bed.

Lew was silent for a moment, then he asked Ada to come to the big house to cook breakfast. Ada said okay, then said that she would be there right away. Lew gave her a hug, turned and walked out of the door. He had only looked at Robert once while in the house. He didn't like to see him hurt and bleeding. He then thought to himself, Robert wouldn't have treated him like that. He would have to go back. Then he noticed the slaves in the fields. Ada came out of her house. Lew told her to go on ahead. He headed for the fields. When he got there, he told the slaves that it was Sunday, and that they all had Sundays off again. They all stopped what they were doing and without a word, headed back to their houses.

On his way back, Lew returned to Ada's house to check on Robert again. As he opened the door, he noticed Old Jordan sitting next to Robert's bed. He patted Robert's forehead with a wet rag as Robert laid there trembling. Lew looked at Robert's face, and tears started coming from his eyes. His green-blue eyes couldn't hold back the water as he stood there, silently looking at his best friend. Robert's face was filled with purple bruises and black scabs from the beating. Lew could see the tears coming from his eyes. Robert was crying. Lew asked Old Jordan how one person could do this to another person. Old Jordan told him that he didn't know as he continued to pat Robert's forehead and wipe away Robert's tears.

Lew couldn't take staying there any longer, and told Old Jordan to tell Robert that he had come by. As he turned to go out the door, Robert called his name. Lew turned around and stood by the bed. Old Jordan got up from the chair, and Lew sat down.

"Yes Rob, I'm here," Lew said.

"In the wildflower field," Robert said. Then he passed out again.

Lew just sat there looking at him. He knew that the field of wildflowers was Robert's favorite place on the plantation. Why did Robert say this? Did he want to go to the field? Well, if that is what he wanted, he would have it.

Lew told Old Jordan to get some men, and later on that day carry Robert outside to the wildflower field. Then he walked out of the house and closed the door behind him. As he walked away from the house, he wiped the tears from his eyes and said to himself, "Robert will make it. He's a survivor."

Lew went in the big house to tell Ada what Robert had said, and what he had told Old Jordan to do. He asked her if it was all right. She said it was. Lew went to talk with his father. He asked him when he had seen Robert. Master Jones said that he hadn't had time to go to see him, but would do it later that day. Lew thought this was odd. He knew his father cared a lot for Robert, yet he hadn't gone to see about him. Lew told his father that he had to come up with a better excuse than that. He told him that he had had plenty of time and demanded to know why he hadn't checked on Robert.

Lew looked at his father's hazel eyes and saw sadness. He saw the same sadness that he saw in Robert's eyes. Then Master Jones told him that he was ashamed. He was ashamed that he had let this happen, ashamed that he had let Isaac treat the slaves the way he had. He was ashamed that he didn't speak up when he knew that Robert hadn't lied. He was ashamed that he did all of this to keep his wife happy, the wife who was upstairs hiding and fearing for her life. Even more so, he was ashamed that he had lost the respect of his only son. Lew hugged his father, told him that he forgave him, and assured him that the others on the plantation would also. He asked him to go see Robert and to talk to the slaves. Master Jones said he would then went into the kitchen.

The smell of Ada's biscuits filled the house. Smiling, Master Jones and Lew sat down to eat. And that was when Mrs. Jones started. She began yelling and screaming as if she had lost her mind.

"I know that nigger Ada is in my house. I know what her cooking smells like, and I can smell it. Get her out of my house!" she yelled.

Master Jones looked at Lew and said, "I've had enough of this."

He walked up the stairs towards her bedroom. Mrs. Jones ran back inside when she saw him coming up the steps. Master hurried behind her, grabbed her by the shoulders, and said, "I love you, and would do anything in this world for you, but this is going to stop, and stop right now. Ada will come in this house to cook and clean. If you don't want to eat it, you don't have to. If you want to keep hiding like some animal, that's all right to. It's all left up to you."

Then Master Jones went back downstairs and ate his breakfast. Mrs. Jones went to her bedroom door. She looked down the hallway leading to the staircase. She thought about losing her son Isaac and the fact that her son Lew wasn't talking to her. Now she was losing her husband, and it was all because of Ada and Robert. It was all their fault. All of the trouble in her life was because of them. Mrs. Jones wasn't going to have this. She wasn't going to let Ada take away her husband.

"I'm not having it," she yelled. "Those niggers are not going to destroy my marriage."

Her cold blue eyes filled with rage and hatred. She grabbed the knife that she had kept hidden in her room, then started towards the stairs. Anger replaced the fear she had felt as she moved towards the steps. When she placed her foot on the first step, her head started spinning and she lost her balance. She let out a scream and fell head-first down the steps. Master Jones, Ada and Lew all ran out of the kitchen to find her laying at the bottom of the stairs. She didn't move or make a sound. The knife that she had been holding was on the floor next to her.

Master Jones picked up her lifeless body and held her in his arms. He told Lew to go into town and get the doctor. Lew ran out of the front door and to the barn to get his horse. Master Jones carried his wife back up to her bedroom. Ada had returned to the kitchen and he called for her to bring some cool wet towels to put them on his wife's forehead. Ada got the towels, wet them, then took them to Mrs. Jones' bedroom.

As she walked in the door, Ada looked at Master Jones. She saw tears on his face. She put her hands on his shoulder and told him that everything would be all right. Then she turned and looked at Mrs. Jones on the bed with her eyes wide open. Ada didn't see anything in her eyes. The coldness and the hate were gone and there was nothing in them. Ada knew at once that she was dead. Ada didn't say another word. She just turned around slowly and walked out the door. As she walked down the steps and back to the kitchen, she wondered why Master Jones hadn't seen this. He had to know that his wife was dead. Master Jones didn't know. He sat next to her, talking to her and patting her forehead with the cool wet towels.

About two hours had passed when Lew returned with the doctor. They went upstairs, and that's when the doctor told them both that she was dead. Then the doctor closed her eyes and pulled the bed sheet over her head. Master Jones started crying loudly as he threw his body across hers and held his wife. He told her that he loved her, and then he looked up and asked God why. He asked God why he had taken her away from him. That's when Lew began to cry. He loved his mother very much. He didn't like the person she had become but she was still his mother and he loved her. So he cried because of his loss. It seemed as if he had been crying all day. First for his friend Robert, and now for his mother.

Some saw the doctor as he was leaving and he told them what had happened. The news of Mrs. Jones' death spread fast around the plantation. The slaves wanted to gather in front of the big house, and they would have at any other time. However, Master Jones had told them all not to come near the house or they would be shot. So the slaves went on about their business just as if nothing ever happened.

Lew walked out of the house and headed for the field of wildflowers. This was Robert's and his favorite place. In the field, he could think, and he would feel better. His heart was filled with pain, and he just wanted to scream. Lew walked out into the field then laid down in the flowers. He turned over onto his back, looked up at the clouds, and let out a loud scream. He did it again and again until he felt calmer and stronger. Then he laid there and looked at the beauty of the flowers and everything around him. All at once, he heard some noise and sat up.

Lew saw some of the slaves coming towards him. They were carrying Robert, bringing him to the field of wildflowers. Lew had forgotten that he had told them to do this. However, now he was glad that he had. The slaves had Robert on a small cot with handles on the sides, which made it easy to carry. Lew asked them to sit the cot next to him. The slaves told Lew that they were all sorry to hear about the loss of his mother. They also told him that they wanted to gather in front of the big house but were afraid to because of Master Jones' warning. Lew said that he understood and thanked them.

As they sat the cot down, Lew noticed that Robert was awake. He smiled at him and said jokingly, "What took you so long to get here?"

Robert looked as if he was trying to smile, but he didn't. Lew asked the other slaves to leave the two of them alone. As they all left, Lew sat closer to Robert's cot. Lew told Robert about Mrs. Jones. He also told Robert how much he missed not being able to talk with him every day. He told Robert about how he had almost killed Isaac, and how Isaac had left the plantation. Then, after a while, he noticed that Robert had gone back to sleep. Robert hadn't done any talking at all. Still, Lew knew that he had enjoyed spending time in the wildflower field.

Lew called for the slaves to come get Robert. He remained sitting in the field as they took Robert home. Lew felt an emptiness inside. He had never felt like this in his life. He didn't know what to do, so he just stayed in the field until it became dark. He told himself that he was glad that this day was over. Then he got up and slowly walked back home.

When he went back in the house, Ada was waiting for him. She called him to the kitchen, and asked him to sit down. She had prepared his supper and wanted to talk with him. Ada placed a plate of food in front of him, then asked him how was his talk with Robert.

"Fine, but I did most of the talking."

Then she asked him what he was feeling. Lew told her that all he felt was emptiness. Ada looked into his beautiful green-blue eyes, walked over to him, and said, "I don't see how a person with so much love in his heart could ever feel empty."

She put her arms around him, hugged him, and then kissed him on the forehead. As she walked out the door, he told her not to worry about cleaning up after him because he would wash his own plate when he finished eating.

Lew ate his food, washed his plate, locked the kitchen door, and went upstairs. He went to his mother's bedroom and found his father still sitting by her bed. The room was dark, so Lew lit a candle and an oil lantern. He stood next to his father, put his hand on his shoulder, and asked him if he was all right. Master Jones said no. He said that this was his fault. He said that he could have done something to prevent it. Lew didn't see how he could have, but he didn't say anything to his father. Still, he knew that it wasn't all his father's fault. Then Master Jones told Lew that Isaac would have to be informed about his mother. He asked Lew to go into town the next morning and tell the people at the Confederate headquarters so that Isaac could come to the burial. Lew told him that he would, then went to his bedroom.

Lew remembered that he had told Isaac that he would kill him. He didn't want Isaac back on the Woodloe Plantation, but now that their mother had died Lew felt that Isaac needed to come back, but only for a day. Isaac would have to leave right after the funeral. He couldn't spend a single night at Woodloe Plantation.

CHAPTER 12

▼

A full moon came out that night. Ada looked at it as she walked to her house. When she got inside she asked Old Jordan how things were going with her son.

"Fine," he replied.

Then she walked over to Robert and asked him how he was feeling. Robert didn't answer his mother. To her, he didn't seem fine at all but seemed to be getting worse. Ada felt his forehead. He was burning up with fever. Old Jordan had said this fever would come, and it had. He also knew that Robert would have to fight it, and it wasn't going to be an easy fight. Old Jordan called for some men to help him pick Robert up, and take him to the river. They would place him in the cool water of the river. This would help him to fight the fever.

Ada started crying as the men walked away carrying her son. Then she remembered people talking about an old woman who lived on the plantation. People said she was a healer. Her name was Miss Lizzy. She was said to be over a hundred years old. No one hardly ever saw her because she stayed in her house, pretty much to herself.

It was said that she came out mostly at night and worked Voo Doo. This didn't matter to Ada. What mattered to her was finding a way to make Robert better. She went to Lizzy's house to ask for help. She would do anything to save the life of her only child.

When Ada walked up to the front door of Lizzy's house, Miss Lizzy said, "Come in Ada." This both surprised and scared Ada because she hadn't even knocked on the door, and she hadn't told Miss Lizzy that she was coming to her home. Ada slowly opened the door and walked into the house. She saw Miss Lizzy seated at a table with a single candle on it. Ada noticed that the house was unusually clean. There were dried flowers hanging on the walls. She also noticed a lot of bottles on the shelves. All types and different sized bottles, maybe fifty or sixty of them. She also saw lots of candles and bowls with powders in them.

"Have a seat," Miss Lizzy told her. "You worried about your boy Robert, but worry can't help him." Then she stood up and reached for a bottle of oil, and said "Yes, this is the one. The whip cut him deep. It not only cut skin and bone, it cut down inside the boy soul. I can heal the skin and bone, but I can't heal the soul."

She gave the bottle to Ada and told her to rub it on Robert's body. Lizzy also told Ada only to rub it on him at night, then bury the bottle in the ground and let it stay there during the day. Ada didn't know why Miss Lizzy told her this, but she would do it, she would do anything to save her son's life. Ada asked Miss Lizzy what she owed her. Miss Lizzy smiled and told her that the next time she made biscuits, to bring her six of them. Ada agreed and thanked Miss Lizzy. As Ada started to walk out of the door, Miss Lizzy told her to try not to worry so much.

Ada went back to her house and waited for the men to bring Robert home. She walked back and forth holding the bottle of oil in her hand. She kept saying to herself, "He's going to be all right, he's going to be all right." After about an hour of this, Ada heard the men coming back. She ran to the door and opened it. Old Jordan and the other men put Robert back in the bed. His fever had broken. He had beaten it for now. Ada told the men thank you, and then she told Old Jordan and the other men to go home and get some rest. She told them that Robert and her would be all right. She didn't tell anyone about her visit to Miss Lizzy's house.

When the men had gone, Ada opened the bottle and started rubbing the oil from it on Robert's body. She rubbed from head to toe, front and back. Then as instructed, she buried the bottle in the yard in front of her house. When Ada came back into the house, she could smell the oil, it smelled sweet and filled the house with its smell. Ada looked at Robert and saw that he was asleep, so she got into her bed and went to sleep. Oh, but sleep was hard to come by for Ada and that night she barely got any. She just kept saying, "My Lord, please help him," over and over again.

The next morning Lew jumped out of his bed, got dressed and headed straight for Ada's house. He had to see how Robert was doing. Ada told him about the fever that Robert had, then she told him that he was all right for now. However, she wasn't sure if he would make it or not. He told Lew that she was afraid, very afraid. Lew gave Ada a hug and told her that he was on his way to inform Isaac about their mother. He said that Robert would be all right and headed out of the door.

"Good bye," said Ada.

Lew turned and told her, "He will be all right Mama Ada. I'll see you when I get back. Bye." Then he headed for the barn.

When Lew reached the barn, he saw two slaves working there. Lew took a key from his pocket and opened the large toolbox at the back of the barn. From it he took out two shovels and an ax and gave them to one of the men. He told them to dig a grave under the magnolia tree that stood on the west side of the plantation, at the end of the wild flower field. Lew got on his horse and rode toward town.

When Lew got into town, he saw soldiers everywhere, more than he had ever seen in his life. He asked one of them where the Confederate headquarters were located. The soldier told him that the courthouse was now the Confederate headquarters. Lew rode down Bull Street and tied his horse to a hitching post in front of the building then went inside. The first thing that Lew noticed was a large flag on the wall near the entrance. It was red, white and blue with a cross of stars on it. Lew had never seen this flag before, so he asked one of the soldiers what kind of flag it was. The soldier told him that it was the flag of the new South, the Confederate flag. Then the soldier asked him if he had come to join the army. Lew told him no, that he just wanted someone to inform his brother Isaac about their mother's death. The soldier told Lew to go to a room down the hall, and the soldier in there would help him.

Lew found the room. A soldier sat behind a larger desk writing. The soldier looked up and asked, "Can I help you?" Lew told him about his mother, and that he wanted to make sure that his brother knew.

"What's your brother's name," the soldier asked.

"Isaac Thurman," Lew replied. "He joined less than a week ago."

The soldier looked in a notebook on his desk and found Isaac's name. "Yes here he is, he's one of Hooker's boys. I'll get the message to him."

The soldier then asked Lew where he lived. Lew told him on Woodloe Plantation just south of Savannah. The soldier then informed him that all of the plantations and farms had to donate food to the army to help feed the soldiers. Lew told the soldier he would have to talk to his father about this and asked the soldier if he could wait until after the funeral. The soldier agreed and said he would send someone out to the plantation after a week.

Lew then walked out of the door and mounted his horse. On his way out of town, he decided to stop at the general store. As soon as he entered the store, two men sitting on the front porch came inside behind him. The two men started laughing and pointing. Then one of them asked, "You one of them Jones' boys from Woodloe Plantation aren't you?"

"Yes, I am Lew Jones."

The two men laughed as Lew looked at them with a blank expression on his face. Then one of the men asked, "How's that nigger brother of yours?"

Lew's face became tight and his eyes narrowed as he asked him what he was talking about.

"That nigger boy, with the same color eyes as your father, Master Jones. Most of us at least hide or sell off our nigger babies, but your pa brought his into town a while back for everyone to see. He sure must to proud of that nigger."

Lew said nothing, walked out of the store, got on his horse and rode off as the two men stood on the porch pointing and laughing. As Lew rode slowly down Bull Street, his mind was racing. These two men were just poor white trash, they didn't know what the hell they were talking about. But he was angry about what had just happened and had to ask himself why. Then Lew thought about what they had said about Robert's eyes. They were the same color as his father's eyes. No one else on the plantation had eyes that color. Even his own were nothing like his father's nor his mother's. Also, Robert never could get anybody to tell him about his father. Why hadn't anyone ever said anything about this?

Then Lew remembered Robert talking about the two white men that had questioned him when he went into town with his father. Lew needed some answers to all of these questions and Robert needed answers also. Last but not least, maybe this was the reason his mother had never wanted Robert in the house. She knew all the time, but never said anything.

When Lew returned to Woodloe he went into the house and looked for his father. He knew that some slave masters had children by their slaves, and he had no reservations about this. The thing that made him angry was that no one was told about it. Robert and he were brothers, blood kin brothers and neither one of them knew it.

Master Jones was in the sitting room where his wife's body was in her casket. A few people were standing around her, talking and telling him how sorry they were for his loss. Lew decided not to say anything for now, he would wait until after the funeral. Lew told his father that the soldiers would contact Isaac, and that the soldier from headquarters would be coming to the plantation for donated food. He spoke to the people standing in the room, then walked down the hall into the kitchen.

Ada and another house slave were cooking food for after the funeral when Lew walked in. Lew looked at her and started to say something, but decided not to. He told her that he was going to go see how Robert was doing. Ada could tell that something was troubling Lew, but she didn't ask him what it was. She asked instead if he was hungry. He said no, and walked out the door.

Lew wondered if everyone on the plantation but Robert and himself knew that Robert was his father's son. As he walked to Ada's house, Lew decided to tell Robert about the two men in the store, and what they had said to him. Old Jordan was sitting with Robert when Lew walked in the house. Lew looked at Robert lying on the bed and saw that he was awake. Good, he thought. Lew asked Old Jordan if he would go to the barn and see about his horse. Old Jordan said yes and walked out the door.

Lew sat in the chair next to Robert's bed. He couldn't help looking at Robert's eyes. "Hazel eyes," he said aloud.

"What?" said Robert.

"You have hazel eyes."

"Yes, I do have hazel eyes. Why'd you sat that?"

Lew asked Robert whom else did he know on Woodloe Plantation with hazel colored eyes.

Robert thought for a moment. There were a lot of slaves who had light complexions like his, and some, like Enoch, were even lighter, but he could think of only one person who had eyes the same color as his.

"Besides me, there's your father ... What about it?"

Lew asked Robert if that seemed a bit odd to him. Robert told him no and asked Lew what he was getting at. Then Lew told Robert about the two men at the store, and what they had said. Robert's face became tight, his eyes drew close together. He shook his head and just said "No."

Lew could see that he had made a mistake by telling him. Maybe he should have waited until Robert was well. Lew could see the pain in his face. Not the pain from the whipping, the pain of finding out that all the people around him had kept this from him all of his life. His own mother, Old Jordan, everyone, and why didn't Master Jones ever say anything about being his father.

"Was he ashamed of me?" Robert asked himself. Then he asked Lew to leave him alone so he could have some time to think.

"Alright, I'll be back later," said Lew, then he left.

Lew walked out of the house and closed the door behind him. He stood there for a moment looking at the big house. Then he heard Robert inside Ada's house. Lew could hear him crying. Lew started to open the door and go back in, but told himself no. As he walked back to the big house, he saw Old Jordan coming from the barn and told him that Robert wanted to be alone for awhile. He asked Old Jordan to check on Robert later. Old Jordan said "yes," and walked on. Lew didn't say anything about this, or about Robert being his brother to anyone that day. He just went inside and greeted the people that came and went all day.

The sun set, and all the people went back to their homes. When Ada got home that night, Robert was sitting up on the bed with his back against the wall. Ada looked at him and said, "You must be feeling better."

Robert looked at her and asked, "Who is my father?"

Ada didn't know why he had asked her that, so she said what she always said. "That's not important, why you thinking about that? The only thing that you need to worry about is getting better."

Robert turned and painfully put both his feet on the floor as he sat on the edge of the bed. He looked up at his mother and started to tell her what Lew had told him. As Robert told the story, tears slowly fell from her big brown eyes, and the more Robert talked the more the tears fell. The pain filled her face. She turned away from Robert so he couldn't see her crying. Then Robert asked her why she had never told him that Master Jones was his father. Ada looked at her son and told him that she had wanted to tell him. So many times in his life she had wanted to, but couldn't for fear that he would be taken away and sold to someone else.

She told him that Master Jones told her that she was never to tell or talk to anyone about it, not even him.

"But I'm your son!" Robert yelled, "I have a right to know who my father is!"

Ada looked at him and said "That might be true, but we are still Master Jones' slaves. The only rights we have is the ones he gives us."

Neither of them said another word that night. Ada tried to rub Robert's wounds, but he went to his pallet and turned away from her. So she let him be and went to bed.

CHAPTER 13

▼

The next morning was the day of Mrs. Jones' funeral. It was to begin at nine o'clock. People had already started to gather in front of the house by the time Lew woke up. He looked out of his bedroom window and wondered if Robert had gotten any better. The he put on a black suit and went downstairs to eat breakfast. When he walked into the kitchen he noticed the look on Ada's face. He could tell that she had been crying, because her eyes were puffy and red. It was as if she felt ashamed to be there. She didn't look Lew in the face, but in a low voice she said, "Morning Lew."

Lew knew then that Robert had told her about Master Jones being his father. Lew walked over to Ada and grabbed her with both hands. He looked her in her big brown eyes and said," Ada, you don't have anything to be ashamed of. Robert is your son and my brother. You don't have any control over that and I know it. All of that was my father's doing, so please don't be ashamed. I love you, I always have and always will Mama Ada. The lady that we are burying today gave birth to me, but you have been more of a mother to me than she ever was."

Then Lew kissed her on the forehead. As he did so, Enoch walked through the back door and tried to look away as he passed through the kitchen. It wasn't very hard for him to guess what Ada was crying about because he always knew that one day she and Robert and young Master Lew would have to face the same situation he had faced many years before. Lew nodded at Enoch, got a cup of coffee, and walked out of the kitchen.

Isaac rode up to the front of the house about the time Lew reached the sitting room. Enoch opened the door for him and a look of surprise came over Isaac's face. For when he had left, Enoch and the other slaves were not allowed in the house. Isaac didn't say anything as he stepped past Enoch. He walked down the hallway and into the sitting room where his mother's body had been placed. Isaac stopped at the door and looked at the people in the room. He was dressed in a Confederate uniform that showed he had been made a lieutenant. A gun and holster hung on his right side, and a sword on the other. His black boots were highly polished, and he stood tall and erect.

Isaac walked over slowly to the casket where his mother laid, bent over and kissed her. Then he took one step backwards and turned around. Not until then did he speak to the people in the room. He walked over to Master Jones who was seated in a high backed chair on the other side of the room. "Sir," he said as he shook Master Jones' hand.

"Hello Isaac," Master Jones said in a quiet voice.

Isaac leaned over and asked, "How did this happen?"

"She fell down the stairs."

Isaac leaned back with a puzzled look on his face, but didn't say anything else. He thought to himself, mother wouldn't go anywhere near the steps, she was afraid to. There's something that he's not telling me. Isaac then walked away and started talking with the guests.

A short time after that, the undertaker announced that it was time to go to the gravesite. He walked over to the casket and closed it. Then six men, friends of Master Jones, picked it up and carried it out the front door. Once outside, they waited for Master Jones, Lew and Isaac to come out of the house, then they walked in a procession to the gravesite. Master Jones right behind the casket, Lew and Isaac behind him, and the guests behind them. Not even one of the slaves was present. They all knew how Mrs. Jones had felt about them because she never hid it. When they reached the gravesite the only slaves there were the two who had to cover the grave after Mrs. Jones was in it. In fact, if they could have helped it, they wouldn't have been there either.

The funeral was a short one. Mrs. Jones was buried in the grave on Woodloe plantation under a big magnolia tree. After her casket was placed in the ground, Master Jones thanked everyone for coming and told them to head back to the house to eat. He said that he wanted to be alone with his wife, and would come home shortly. Lew, Isaac, and the other guests slowly began to walk back towards the house. When they got there, they found that Ada had prepared a feast, and they began to eat. After they all had been fed, some of them went home, and some stayed.

Master Jones came back to the house about half an hour later, and Ada prepared a plate of food for him. As she placed it on the table, he thanked her and told her that he didn't know what he would do without her. Isaac overheard this and gave Ada a nasty look with those cold blue eyes. Ada saw it and thought about Robert. She wanted to tell Master Jones what had happened the night before, but she didn't. She just said thank you and started cleaning the mess that the guests were making.

A short time later, Isaac walked out of the house and retrieved a bag from off his horse. He came back into the house and headed up the stairs to his old bedroom. Lew noticed him as he came back down the steps. Lew started to tell him right then that he was no longer welcome on Woodloe, but decided to wait until after the guests were gone.

However, things didn't work out that way. It seems that Isaac wanted a slice of cake. Since there was no more in the dining room, he decided to go into the kitchen and look for some. When he entered the kitchen Ada was there washing dishes. Isaac told her to get him some cake. She told Isaac that there was no more, but there were pies and sweetbreads. Isaac got mad and called her a "no count nigger," then he kicked her. When Isaac kicked Ada, she fell and hit her face on the sink. The dishes in her hands fell to the floor and broke.

Lew heard the noise from the sitting room. He got up and ran towards the kitchen to see what was going on. As Lew raced down the hallway leading to the kitchen, he saw Isaac coming out of the kitchen door. Lew looked into those cold blue eyes as they passed each other. Lew could see the hate on Isaac's face, the same hate that was there before Isaac went away was back again. Ada was on her knees picking up the broken dishes when Lew walked in.

"What happened?" he asked.

Ada said nothing had happened and continued to pick up the broken dishes. Lew looked at Ada's face and saw the mark where her face had hit the sink. Lew shouted, "That damn Isaac!" and headed out the kitchen. Ada tried to hold him and keep him from saying anything, but he was too strong. Isaac had returned to the dining room when Lew found him. Lew walked over to him and said, "I think it's high time for you to be leaving."

Isaac looked at Lew and in a cold voice said, "Leaving for what, did that nigger back there in the kitchen tell you that I kicked her? Well, she's lying. I did no such thing."

"No," said Lew, "you just told me, now get your things and get out of this house."

"You can't tell me to leave, this is my mother's house."

Lew put his face just inches from Isaac's, looked into his cold blue eyes and said, "Your mother is dead, she doesn't own this house. This is Jones property, and you are not a Jones. So get out before they carry you out."

Master Jones heard all of the commotion and came to see what the problem was. Lew told him that Isaac had kicked Ada, and now he had told him that it was time for him to leave. Isaac said that he did no such thing, and Lew couldn't tell him when to leave because this was his mother's house. Master Jones called Isaac to the side, away from Lew. He told him, "Yes, this was your mother's home, but we have our ways of doing things on Woodloe Plantation. Your way of doing things is not our way, so yes, I think it's time for you to go. You may come and visit your mother's grave anytime that you want to, but you can't stay on Woodloe."

Isaac said in a loud voice, "You bunch of nigger lovers! Let me get the hell away from all of you." He then went upstairs to get his bag.

While he was up there, he went into his mother's room and found the pearls that he had given her. He put them in his pocket, walked back down the stairs and out the front door. Isaac got on his horse and rode away from the house towards the arched gate. He rode past the field of wildflowers and down the dirt road passing the oak trees. He was about halfway down the road when a shot rang out and Isaac fell from his horse. Master Jones and his remaining guests heard the shot. They all rushed to the front porch to see what had happened. They saw Isaac's horse running back towards the house with no one on it. Master Jones looked down the road and saw Isaac laying on the ground in the middle of the road.

Everyone started running down the road towards the spot where Isaac laid. When they reached his body, they realized that Isaac was dead. He had been shot in the head. Everyone looked around, but they didn't see anyone. They wondered who had done this. Master Jones and his guests also realized that the person responsible for Isaac's death was probably long gone by now.

Master Jones asked one of the guests if he would go into town and bring back the marshal. Then he and some of the others picked up Isaac's body and carried him towards the house. As they neared the front door, Lew walked out onto the front porch. He looked at Isaac's body, then looked at his father. They looked into each others' eyes. His father was wondering if Lew had had someone do this terrible thing. After all, he had tried to kill Isaac only days before. Could he have finally finished what he had started?

Lew had just had words with Isaac before he left the house. Besides, where was he when Isaac was shot? Lew knew what his father was thinking, and wondered how his father could ever think that he could do something so vile. Although no words were ever spoken, they both knew what the other was thinking.

An hour had passed when two men came riding down the dirt road. They were Confederate soldiers. Since the South was at war, Savannah was under marshal law. This meant that they would investigate the murder. They rode up to the front porch where Master Jones and Lew met them. The guests that was still there remained inside the house. The two soldiers looked at the wound, talked to each other for a moment or two, then covered Isaac's body back up with the sheet that Master Jones had placed over him.

One of the soldiers asked Master Jones what had happened. He told him that Isaac was leaving the plantation, riding down the road, when he was shot. The soldiers asked if anyone had seen it when it happened. Master Jones told them no, and that everyone was inside of the house. Then one of the soldiers told Master Jones that the bullet had come from a rifle used by Union soldiers. He also informed Master Jones that there had been reports of Union soldiers in the area. After speaking to Master Jones, one of the soldiers took the gun, holster, sword, and boots off of Isaac's body. After this was done, the soldiers told Master Jones that they were sorry about the loss of his son.

Master Jones stood there wondering how the men could just look at a wound and know what kind of weapon it had come from. One of the soldiers then told Master Jones about the food that he wanted for the army. Master Jones looked at the soldier and wondered how he could be so cold. Isaac's dead body was lying right there in front of them both, and this solider was acting as if nothing had ever happened. Master Jones asked him to come back the next day and then they would discuss it. With that, both of the soldiers got on their horses and rode off. Isaac was buried that same day, and his grandparents were sent a telegram informing them of his death. He was placed in a grave next to his mother. The only people that were present were Master Jones, Lew, the undertaker, and the two slaves that dug the grave.

CHAPTER 14

▼

Robert had heard about Isaac and wanted to see if the rumor of his death was true. His heart was filled with anger and confusion as he thought of how only a few days before this man had tried to kill him. He never did know the reason why Isaac had beat him so badly. However, he was glad that someone else instead of him had killed Isaac and he couldn't help wondering who had done it. Robert just told himself, "You get back what you give." Still, he had more pressing things than Isaac to think about. He needed to confront Master Jones. He had to look him in his eyes and ask him if he was his father. And if he was, why did he keep it from him for all these years?

Robert got out of his bed and stood up. He decided that he would go to the big house and talk to Master Jones. He was hurt that Master Jones hadn't come to see about him. Robert thought that Master Jones cared more about animals on the plantation than he did about his own blood kin. Not even after he knew about the beating, and how Isaac tried to kill him did Master Jones set one foot inside of Ada's house to see about him.

"If he is my father, he's one cold hearted man," Robert said aloud.

Robert started walking toward the door. He took one step. The pain shot down his back and into his legs. Robert took another step, and with that one he fell to the floor. He screamed out in pain as he lay on the floor. He would have to wait until he was stronger to confront Master Jones. He stayed on the floor for a few minutes, then dragged himself back over to his pallet.

As he lay on the pallet, he started to ask himself questions. Why didn't Master Jones want me to know that he is my father? Am I that bad of a person? Is he ashamed of me? How did it happen in the first place? Did he rape my mother, and if he did I'll kill him. The more he thought, the more questions he had. His mind began to spin, and his head began to hurt. Finally, Robert went to sleep, and allowed himself to enjoy some peace.

When Ada walked into the house that night, Robert woke up. He had some questions to ask her.

"How you feeling today," she asked as she rubbed him with the oil she had gotten from Miss Lizzy.

"I'll be all right," Robert replied.

Ada had brought him some of the supper from the big house. When she finished rubbing him with the oil, she handed it to him in bed.

Robert looked up at her and asked, "Did Master Jones rape you? Is that why you didn't want me to know that he is my father?"

Ada looked down at her son and took a deep breath. She paused for a moment then said, "Son, some things in life we have to let go of. Now that you know that he is your father, let it go."

Ada picked up the two pots from the stove, the small bottle of oil, and walked out the door. When she returned with the water to wash her uniform, she told Robert not to say another word, and she said nothing else that night herself.

The next morning Lew got out of bed early. He walked over to his bedroom window and took a look out. He saw some of the slaves walking around, getting ready for the start of another workday. He would go and see about them later. First, he had to talk to his father. He got dressed and went downstairs to the breakfast room. His father hadn't got up yet, so Lew went to the kitchen, where he found Ada cooking breakfast.

"Morning Ada, how's everything," he asked.

Ada looked at him, smiled and said, "Fine, but I'm worried about Robert."

Lew sat down at the big table in the kitchen, and told Ada that he would have a talk with his father in a little while. However, there was something that he had to do first. Lew got his breakfast and sat with Ada while he ate it. When he finished, he kissed her on the forehead and walked out towards the barn.

Two slaves were tending to the needs of the animals in the barn when Lew walked in. He went over to the big box where all of the tools were locked. He opened it, then told the two slaves to tell everyone to come get the tools they needed to do their work. After doing this, Lew went back into the house to talk with his father.

"Have some breakfast with me," Master Jones said quietly.

Lew told him that he had already eaten. He then told him that he had given the tools back to the slaves. He asked his father if this was all right with him.

Master Jones said that he had no problem with it. With that out of the way, Lew began to tell his father about the two men at the general store, and what they had said to him. As Lew talked he could see his father's face growing tight. His eyes came close together, and all at once he shouted, "Damn them, they had no right!"

Lew just looked at his father. He knew then that everything was true. Right then and there Lew knew that Robert was his brother, his older brother because Robert was born two hours before him. Lew then asked his father why he hadn't told Robert that he was his father. Master Jones was quiet for a while before answering, "Because it's just the way things are done."

Lew stood up and headed for the door, then he turned around and said, "Well Robert knows. And you need to talk to him. I know that if he were strong enough he would be here talking to you."

With that said, Lew walked out of the room. He was headed down the hall when he heard Enoch announce that there were riders in front of the house. They were the Confederate soldiers coming to get the supplies they had requested. Lew called his father, and they both walked out onto the front porch. There were five soldiers, three on horseback and two in a wagon. A sergeant named Danny Mills got off of his horse and walked up onto the porch.

"Morning sir," said Sergeant Mills as he brushed the dust from his uniform.

"Morning," replied Master Jones.

Sergeant Mills then handed Master Jones a list of things he wanted. Master Jones looked at the list and said, "Okay, we will have these things for you in a little while."

He gave the list to Lew and told him to have some of the slaves gather the things on it. Sergeant Mills told Master Jones that they would return once a month for more supplies to help feed the troops. Once everything had been gathered and loaded on the wagon, the sergeant thanked Master Jones. He and the other soldiers then left. Both Lew and Master Jones seemed to be glad to see them leave. It just didn't feel right for Confederate soldiers to be on Woodloe Plantation.

Things pretty much returned to normal on the plantation following the visit of the confederate soldiers. Master Jones never did go see Robert. Maybe he didn't care to, or maybe it was pride, or even guilt that was keeping him away. What ever it was, he never set one foot into Ada's house to see about Robert.

CHAPTER 15

―――――――――▼―――――――――

A month passed and Robert grew stronger each day. Old Lizzy's oil had done its job. The slaves were all happy again, and the plantation was doing well. Aside from hearing gun shots in the distance every once in a while, you could hardly tell there was a war going on. In fact, things might have been a little too perfect on Woodloe. Perhaps that is why the soldiers came and did what they did.

One day Sergeant Mills and six men came to Woodloe. This time they had two wagons instead of one. The sergeant gave Master Jones a list of needed items then told him the army needed some of his slaves.

"For what?" asked Master Jones, looking at the sergeant with surprise.

Sergeant Mills explained that the army was building roads on the riverfront in Savannah and the slaves would be used to do the labor. Master Jones asked him how many he needed and Sergeant Mills answered twenty. Master Jones just stood there and shook his head as if he was saying no. Then Sergeant Mills said something Master Jones had not expected: he told him he had known Isaac, and that the slaves of Woodloe Plantation had been chosen because Isaac had bragged about how well they worked and how they all feared him. There was nothing Master Jones could do but call all the slaves together. So he got the big cowbell and rang it.

All the slaves gathered in front of the house except for Robert, Lizzy, and the house slaves. Enoch looked out the window from behind a curtain to see what was going on. When they saw the soldiers and the two wagons, they all knew that something was wrong. However, none of them knew what it was. As they stood in front of the big house, Master Jones told them that twenty of them would be working in town to help build roads. This frightened most of them because they had never been away from Woodloe Plantation. Then right out of the blue, the soldiers started pushing and hitting the men that they wanted as they forced them to get into the wagons. The women and children of the men's families started crying as the twenty slaves were loaded onto the wagons.

After Sergeant Mills and the other soldiers got the men they wanted, Master Jones asked the sergeant how long they would be gone.

"I don't know for sure, but you'll get'em back."

Lew, seeing how the soldiers had treated the slaves, spoke out and said, "Yes, but in what condition will they be returned?"

Sergeant Mills just laughed and got on his horse. As the slaves rode away from the plantation, the ones left behind couldn't help but worry about them. Slaves at Woodloe generally stayed on the plantation their entire lives and rarely separated from each other for any reason other than a short trip to town. And they had already seen how these soldiers mistreated them even before they left Woodloe. They all knew that the treatment would get worse. You could see the fear in the eyes of each slave as they rode down the long dirt road and out of sight. Little did they know that some of them would never return to Woodloe.

After the soldiers departed, the remaining slaves went back to work, Master Jones went back into the house, and Lew went to see Robert to tell him what had just occurred. Robert had started to walk again. He could only take a few steps at a time, but every day he took more steps than the day before. Lew told Robert about the soldiers, and how they had treated the men. He said he was worried about them. They both knew there was nothing that could be done about it. It was just another part of this awful war, along with all of its killing and hatred. It was sucking the life out of the South and everyone that lived in the South. It had changed everybody in some way or another. Robert had been changed by the way Master Jones started treating him and the other slaves after Isaac first came to Woodloe. And the beating Isaac had given him changed not only Robert but all of the slaves on Woodloe.

The fact that he found out Master Jones was his father didn't sit too well with him either. Robert knew that he had to let go of all the things that were crowding his mind. He also knew that if he kept thinking about them he would soon go mad. So, he made up his mind that as soon as he was strong enough to get around, he would walk right into the front door of the big house, have a seat in the sitting room, and have a good long talk with his father, Master Jones.

Another month passed, and every once in a while the people on Woodloe could hear the gun shots coming from a distance. The Confederate soldiers would come to get their supplies and leave. They would never tell anyone when the slaves would be returned. They would just say, "as soon as we get finished with them." Upset over the lack of information given by the soldiers, Lew decided to go into town to see for himself how they were getting along. He told his father and Robert that he was going to check on them. Lew and Old Jordan loaded some things to sell at the farmers market and headed for town.

Once they reached the city, Lew realized that Savannah had changed a lot. There were more people in the city than he had ever seen before. They were everywhere, running back and forth. They all seemed to be in some kind of a hurry. Soldiers were everywhere you looked. You could hardly walk down the street without tripping over one of them. Lew told Old Jordan not to leave his side while they were in town. He didn't feel that Old Jordan would be safe by himself. The two of them reached the market. Old Jordan pulled the wagon in front of the warehouse. They both went inside, and Lew told the warehouse clerk what he had to sell. After a little negotiating, they both agreed on a selling price. When that was over, Lew and Old Jordan started unloading the wagon. They put all the cargo on the loading dock, and Lew got his money. Before they left, Lew asked the clerk if he knew where the slaves were working on the streets. Lew was told to go down to the riverfront and he would find them. Lew told Old Jordan to head north to Bay Street and start looking for them.

As they rode, they saw hundreds of slaves. The soldiers had them doing all kinds of work, from cutting grass to pulling loaded wagons like horses. Lew then told Old Jordan to go to the riverfront. They started at the east end, and headed west. The street had been paved with large stones. There were lots of ships docked on the edge of the street, with slaves working to load and unload each one of them. Suddenly, Old Jordan saw one of the slaves from Woodloe. He called out his name. The man looked up and saw Lew and Old Jordan. He looked very happy to see them as he ran towards their wagon.

"Help me!" he shouted. "Please help me!"

As he grabbed the side of the wagon, Lew noticed that his body was scarred with cuts from whippings. He looked as if he had barely been eating. He was just skin and bones. A soldier hit the man with a whip.

"Nigger, I didn't tell you to stop working," he said. Lew jumped down from the wagon and grabbed the whip. The soldier looked at Lew and asked him what he thought he was doing. Lew told him that this slave was his and he didn't like the way he was being treated. Then Lew demanded to see the rest of his slaves. The soldier told Lew he would have to talk with his commanding sergeant and get permission from him. Although Lew didn't like the fact that he had to do this in order to talk to his own slaves, he agreed. Lew told the man to go back to work, and to tell the others that he would be back to see about them.

Lew told Old Jordan to stay in the wagon while he walked to the sergeant's tent. It was just a little further down the road. He would be right back. As Lew walked, he was able to see for himself just what was happening to his slaves. He couldn't help but notice that most of them looked half dead, and all of them had been beaten. They were underfed and looked sickly. The clothes they wore were no more than dirty rags and they looked as if they hadn't bathed in weeks. Despite this, white people would come to the riverfront to watch them. The very thought of this made Lew sick to his stomach. Why would people want to watch other people suffering?

Finally, he reached the sergeant's tent, and asked for the sergeant in charge. He assumed it would be Sergeant Mills but it wasn't. A tall fat man came out of the tent and introduced himself as Sergeant Colbert. He asked Lew who he was and what he wanted. Lew told him and said he wanted to see his slaves to talk with them. Sergeant Colbert went back into his tent and returned after a few minutes with a large book in his hand. He found the page with the Woodloe Plantation on it. He then told Lew that five of the twenty slaves were dead, but he could talk with the others. Then the sergeant told a private to go and get the slaves. He could find them by the numbers that they were all given when they first arrived there. Lew told the private that he would go with him because he didn't need numbers, he knew their names. Lew thanked the sergeant and headed back to the spot where he had left Old Jordan with the wagon.

As Lew walked back with the private, he asked him if he knew how his slaves had died. The private jokingly said, "Some niggers don't take a beating too well, and others don't swim too well," then laughed. Lew just looked at him and continued to walk. He remembered that first lesson he had learned in school as a boy. When he reached the wagon, he asked Old Jordan if he was all right. Old Jordan answered yes.

Then Lew asked the private to bring his slaves to the wagon. They waited by the wagon, and one by one the slaves walked over to them. Every single one of them was dirty and sickly looking. They all told Lew about the mistreatment; how the soldiers had killed some slaves and let others die. They told him how the slaves had to carry loads of large stones for the road from the ships. They had to carry these across narrow planks, and if they fell into the Savannah River, they would be swept away by the currents and drown. The soldiers could place nets under the planks, but choose not to. In any case, the soldiers would just stand around and watch, laughing and joking as the slave pounded the water in a desperate fight for his life. One of the slaves showed Lew his back. He had been badly beaten and this made Lew think about Robert. Lew was already angry and this made him even more upset.

"That's it," he told them. "I'm taking all of you back home."

He told them all to get into the wagon, then he told Old Jordan to drive to the sergeant's tent. Once at the tent, Lew asked for Sergeant Colby. When the sergeant came out of his tent, he saw the slaves in the back of the wagon and told them to get out. Lew told them to stay seated and reminded the sergeant that they belonged to him. Sergeant Colby told Lew there was a war going on and he was under marshal law. Lew told him the law didn't make provisions to take a man's property, then asked if he was going to be paid for the slaves he had lost. The sergeant stood silent for a moment, and then said that he didn't know.

"Well I'm not willing to lose any more of my slaves and I'm taking them home."

"You'll have to get permission from the captain at headquarters to do that," Said Sergeant Colby.

"Fine," said Lew, then told the sergeant to follow the wagon to Bull Street where headquarters was located. Lew got back into the wagon and rode with Old Jordan to the Confederate headquarters. Nobody in the wagon said a single word while they drove towards Bull Street. The slaves were afraid they would not make it back home. They knew the soldiers had power, and this was enough to convince them that they would stay. Besides, they knew first-hand how the soldiers worked and what they were capable of. When they pulled up in front of the confederate headquarters building, Lew told all the slaves to stay in the wagon and not say anything to anyone.

The sergeant and Lew walked into the building as the slaves watched in silence. It seemed as if Lew had been gone for about an hour. However, when he came out, he got in the wagon and told Old Jordan to head for home. The slaves in the back of the wagon let out a loud cheer and laughed and hugged each other. Some of the men started to cry because they were finally getting away from the cruelty of the soldiers that had the power of life and death over them. Lew just sat in the wagon and didn't say anything the whole time they traveled toward Woodloe.

When the wagon pulled in front of the big arched gate at Woodloe Plantation, one of the slaves asked if he could walk down the dirt road that led to the big house. Lew said yes, and Old Jordan stopped the wagon for him to get out. Then the rest of the slaves got out without saying a word. Lew and Old Jordan drove on ahead of the men. Old Jordan pulled in front of the big house. Lew got out the wagon and went into the house, looking for his father to hell him what had happened with the slaves. Old Jordan took the wagon to the barn and told some of the slaves that the men were coming down the road.

Lew couldn't find his father, so he came back outside and rang the big cowbell to call all the slaves to the big house. When the slaves on the plantation heard the bell, they all came running and stood in front of the house. Lew told them that the men were coming down the road. They all stood there and watched as the men walked slowly towards them. When they had reached the front of the house, all of the slaves ran to the men and hugged them. The fact that they were dirty and smelled badly didn't matter so much because everyone was glad to see them back home. But it was a bittersweet moment too because of the five men who had not returned. Realizing this, some of the slaves started to cry. The pain of seeing this went through Lew's body, but there was nothing he could do about it. He told the men to come to the barn to get some new clothes. He also told the slaves that tomorrow would be a day of celebration. Lew then told each of the men that had returned that they had a full week to rest and to regain their strength.

When he was finished, Lew went back to the big house where he told Ada to prepare a feast for the men. Then he asked her if she knew where his father was. She told him Master Jones was in his bedroom taking a nap. Lew went to his father's room and called out to him.

"Father," he said, "I have something important to tell you."

Master Jones sat up on the edge of his bed and asked, "What is it son?" He knew by the look in his son's eyes that something was very wrong.

Lew told his father that he had just joined the army.

"No!" shouted Master Jones. "Why in God's name would you do something like that?"

Lew then began to tell his father about the conditions in which he had found the slaves and about the mistreatment he had witnessed first hand. He told his father how the soldiers had killed some of them and let the others die as they stood around and joked about it. Lew said that when he went to the Confederate headquarters to inform the captain that he wanted his slaves, the captain refused to release them and said the army was not going to pay for the slaves that were lost. That was when he and the captain came to the agreement that the slaves would come home if Lew joined the army.

"I was not coming back without them," Lew said, looking into his father's hazel eyes.

Master Jones let out a long sigh, then he rubbed his face with his hands and said, "Well I guess you did what you felt you had to do son."

"Yes sir."

Lew told his father he would be leaving in two days, and then walked out the room. Master Jones stood up and walked over to his bedroom window. He stood there looking out as tears fell silently from his eyes. He had already lost so much, he just couldn't bear the thought of loosing Lew.

Lew left the house and went to see Robert. When he arrived, he found Robert sitting in front of his cabin on a wooden box.

"How we doing today boy?" Lew said as he smiled at his brother.

"I'm getting stronger by the day old man," Robert replied, "and pretty soon I'll be strong enough to beat you in a foot race."

Lew sat on the ground next to Robert and began telling him about his trip into town. When Lew had finished, he told Robert he had joined the army and explained why. Then he looked at Robert and waited to hear what he had to say. Lew could see the sadness in Robert's eyes. Robert just looked straight ahead, and then at the ground in front of him.

Lew said, "Tell me what you're thinking, say something."

"Just make sure that you bring your hind parts back home in one piece, that all I got to say about it."

They hugged, and Lew stood up and walked back towards the big house. As Lew walked away, Robert said to himself, "I hate this war, and everything that it stands for."

A few moments later, he got up and went inside the cabin.

CHAPTER 16

▼

The next morning when Robert woke up, he could smell the hog cooking. The aroma filled the whole plantation and let everyone know that it was a special occasion, a time to feast and celebrate. As the hog cooked, the tables were set. All of the slaves began to gather on the side of the big house. Some of them played music or sang and others played games. Some just had a good time talking amongst each other. Even Robert went out to enjoy the feast. And those slaves who had lost their loved ones seemed as happy as everybody else. Everyone knew that it would take some time for them to get over their loss. Maybe the feast and being around the men who had made it back home would help. Besides, there was plenty of time for grief later. Today was a day for celebration.

Master Jones and Lew came out of the house around eleven o'clock that morning. Enoch, Ada, and the other house slaves soon followed behind them. Master Jones took his seat at the head of the table with Lew. As he sat there, he looked around and remembered the last time they had all gathered together. It had been to celebrate Lew's birthday. He thought to himself how so much had happened since that day. Master Jones smiled and stood up. He asked the slaves that had come back from Savannah to join him and Lew at the head table. Everyone stopped and looked at Master Jones. He had never invited any of his slaves to eat at the head table, so no one could believe their ears. One by one, the men slowly walked over to the head table and sat down.

Master Jones said, "Let's eat," and the fun began again. The feast lasted long after sundown, and into the night. It was a feast that the slaves would talk about for years to come.

The next morning, the wind blew warm and softly as the birds sang their songs all around the plantation. Most of the slaves stayed in bed and slept late. Lew had told them they could have the day off. Ada woke up before sunrise and had already gone to the big house by the time Robert got up that morning. Robert had sat back at the feast and watched Lew that whole day. Lew didn't have much to say, and wasn't acting like himself. However, no one knew that better than Robert did, for they knew each other inside and out. This had bothered Robert all night. Now the day was coming for Lew to leave for the army.

Robert got dressed and walked over to the big house. He walked in the back door and entered the kitchen where Ada was. He had always been forbidden to enter the house and Ada was surprised to see him when she looked up.

"What's wrong?" she asked him.

Robert smiled and said, "Oh nothing."

He proceeded down the hall and up the staircase towards Lew's room. Ada stood there in shock with her mouth wide open and not saying a word. She couldn't. She thought her son must have lost his mind to come inside the house and walk though it like that. Robert went to Lew's room and closed the door behind him.

"Lew, wake up," he said as he shook him.

Lew slowly opened his eyes and saw Robert standing there. He asked Robert what he wanted.

"I want you to tell me the truth," Robert said.

"What truth? What the hell are you talking about?"

Robert looked right into Lew's eyes and said, "I know you. And there's more to the story than joining the army just because of the slaves."

Lew yawned loudly, then sat up, stretched, and scratched his head. He walked over to a small table where a face bowl sat with water in it. He washed and dried his face, then started to talk.

"You are right, there is more. When I went into the Confederate headquarters, I met with a captain. We talked, and I told him that I had come to take my slaves back home. He told me that I could do no such thing. I reminded him that they belonged to me, and by law, I had the right to do with them as I pleased. He tried to argue this point, but he couldn't. Finally, he told me that I could take them if I wanted to. However, I would have to join the army to replace them and Isaac. He said that if I didn't, he couldn't guarantee that our plantation would be protected from raiders. He told me that the word may even get out that Woodloe Plantation had no protection. I knew what that meant. This whole plantation would be raided and destroyed. Now we both know that I couldn't let that happen, not in this lifetime, not in a hundred years. Now you know why I joined, I had to."

Robert didn't say anything. He just walked out of the room and out of the house. He went into the field of wildflowers where he and Lew had spent so many hours during their childhood. He found a spot in the center of the field and laid down among the flowers. He closed his eyes, and a peaceful feeling came over him. He felt the sun's rays warming his body, and the soft flowers on his back. Suddenly, he heard something. He looked up, and there stood Lew. Lew picked a spot alongside Robert and laid down.

"After all these years, it still feels good to come out here," Lew said.

"Sure does", replied Robert, "It's ashamed the rest of life isn't like this field."

Lew sat up and asked Robert what he meant by that.

"See the flowers? They are all different colors, sizes, and shapes," said Robert. "They are all beautiful by themselves, but all together in one place, they are magnificent."

"They sure are," said Lew as he laid back down.

After about fifteen minutes or so, Robert told Lew that he was going to confront Master Jones today. Lew told him that he had often wondered when he was going to do it. Robert said that he was waiting until he had gotten stronger. Now, since Lew would be leaving tomorrow, Robert figured that he shouldn't wait any longer. Lew asked Robert if he wanted him to be there when he talked with his father.

"No, this is something that I have to do by myself."

Besides, Robert didn't know what he was going to say to Master Jones. All he knew was that he wanted to hear him say that he was his father. He wanted to hear the words come out of Master Jones' own mouth.

Robert got up and headed towards the big house. When he reached it, he did just what he said he would do. He walked right in through the front door, went inside the sitting room, and sat in a high-backed chair. When Enoch saw Robert do this, he ran into the kitchen to tell Ada.

"That boy of yours done lost his mind," he said. "He done walked right in the front door, and is sitting in the Master's sitting room."

Ada looked at him and said, "Well, I guess you better go and get Master, and tell him he has company."

Enoch looked at Ada for a few minuets, then went up the staircase and told Master Jones that Robert was waiting for him in the sitting room. Master Jones took his time coming down, but Robert didn't care, because he wasn't going anywhere until he had his say.

When Master Jones walked in the room, Robert didn't get up from the chair that he was sitting in. Instead, he told Master Jones to have a seat.

Master Jones looked at him and said, "I knew that this day would come when I heard that you found out that I'm your father." Then he sat in a chair facing Robert.

"Well are you my father?" Robert asked.

"Yes," said Master Jones, "I am."

"Why did you keep me from knowing that for all these years?"

Master Jones didn't answer, so Robert said, "You don't even know me. You don't know who, or even what I am."

Master Jones looked into Robert's hazel eyes and said, "But I do know you. I know every slave on this plantation, and I know that you are one of the best on this plantation. I know that Lew taught you to read and write. I know that you have a bible, and I know that you hate me, and I know that I can't blame you for hating me. There's nothing that I can do about that. It's just the way things are. What I did is done. Nothing's going to change that, so you can go on hating, or you can choose to live your life like the boy that I've watched grow up to become a man. A man with a good heart that I'm very proud of.

"Remember years ago when I took you into town with me to the store? I knew you could count your money, but I didn't say anything because you are my son. You don't know of any other slave that can read, write, and count, but you can. I'm proud of that also."

"If you are so proud of all of this, why didn't you come to see about me after Isaac almost beat me to death? I could have died for all you cared."

Master Jones told Robert that he didn't come because it was his fault. He was the one who let Isaac take over the plantation and mistreat the slaves. For this reason, he was ashamed. He then said, "Son, I couldn't bear to see you that way, knowing that I had a part in it."

Robert looked at the old man seated in front of him, and thought to himself, I just don't understand him. Maybe I never will. He wondered if being proud and being ashamed both meant the same thing to Master Jones. Robert got up and said, "I'll talk with you later," and walked out of the room.

Within an hour, the whole plantation was buzzing with the story of what had happened in the big house. By the time the slaves had finished telling it, the whole story had been changed around. Now it was that Master Jones had whipped Robert because he found out that Robert could read and write. This was a lot of silliness, and Robert paid no attention to it. He had his talk with his father, and that was all that mattered. Lew, on the other hand, wanted to know what was said. He had been in the kitchen the whole time, but could not hear a word. He also wanted to know if Robert was all right. He found Robert late that evening down by the river. He was just standing there looking at the water.

"Go ahead and jump in," Lew shouted as he walked towards Robert.

"No, not today, "Robert said as he turned around.

"Well, how did it go? What was said?"

"He told me that he was my father, and that he knew that you taught me how to read and write."

"How's that?!" Lew said loudly with his face balled up.

"Yes, that's what he said, and then he told me that he was proud of me."

"Now don't that just beat all."

Robert stood there looking at Lew and they both started laughing. They talked about how they had tried to hide the fact that Lew had taught Robert the lessons he learned in school. After they both had a good laugh, Robert said he was going to bed and he would see Lew in the morning.

CHAPTER 17

▼

The next morning came quickly, maybe a bit too quickly. Robert didn't get much sleep the night before. For this was the day when Lew would be leaving. No one on Woodloe wanted to see him go. They all thought he was leaving because he had brought the slaves back from town. Only he and Robert knew the full story. Lew had enlisted to save the plantation. It was too many people's home for him not to.

Robert decided to have breakfast with Lew that morning. He got dressed and walked over to the big house. He started to go through the front door but went through the back instead. He said good morning to Ada and the other house slaves in the kitchen, then asked if Lew was up yet. Ada told him no, so he went upstairs to Lew's bedroom. Lew was already awoke and packing the things that he would take with him. He told Robert that he hadn't slept well that night. Robert asked Lew if he could help him pack. Lew answered no because he wasn't taking very much with him. After everything was packed, the two of them went downstairs together. Master Jones was in the breakfast room when Robert and Lew walked in.

"Morning Sir," Robert said as he entered the room.

Master Jones just looked at the both of them and said, "Morning."

Lew and Robert sat down at the table next to each other. Ada hesitated before placing a plate in front of Robert. She looked at Master Jones and he nodded that it was ok for her to fix Robert's breakfast also. They all ate without speaking a single word the whole time. After eating, Master Jones got up and walked outside.

"That went well," Lew said to Robert, and they both began to laugh.

After they had eaten, Lew got up and went into the kitchen. Robert walked out of the back door and disappeared. Lew wanted to say goodbye to Ada and the other slaves. He gave Ada a kiss on the forehead and asked her not to worry. He could see it in her big brown eyes. He told her that he would be back. He also promised to write to Robert to let everyone know how he was doing. With that said, Lew picked up his bag and headed out the kitchen door to get his horse.

As soon as Lew had reached the corner of the house, he could see all the slaves gathered in front of it. His father was standing on the front porch. His horse had already been saddled, and was ready for him. Lew hadn't heard the cowbell ring to call them all together. Still, they all had come to see him off. He smiled and slowly began walking through the crowd of people. Some of them had tears in their eyes, others just smiled as he said goodbye and that he would miss them. As he worked his way through the crowd, he noticed his father on the porch, and Old Jordan standing near the bottom step. Lew walked over to Old Jordan and shook his hand. He told him to take care of his father and Woodloe Plantation. He then walked up onto the porch, hugged his father and said goodbye. He asked him to do right by Robert. Then he turned and faced the slaves standing in front of the house.

Lew said to all of them, "I don't want any of you to worry about me. I know that you don't want to see me leave, but I have to. Believe me when I tell you, I will be back. I want you to take care of yourselves and your home, and before you know it, I'll be back."

After speaking to the slaves, Lew got on his horse and looked around for Robert. He didn't see him anywhere.

"Where's Robert?" he asked.

No one knew, so Lew proceeded to ride down the dirt road. He walked his horse slowly toward the arched gate looking for Robert as he went. He looked in the wildflower field and in the woods on both sides of the road. Still, no Robert to be found. Lew wondered what had happened to him. Finally, when Lew reached the gate, Robert walked out from behind a large oak tree.

"You didn't think I would let you leave without saying goodbye, did you?" Robert asked with a smile.

"Yeah, I did, you had me kind of worried there," Lew replied. Lew got down from his horse and they hugged.

"Well," said Robert, "I'm the last to see you leaving Woodloe and I want to be the first to see you when you get back."

"Don't worry, you will be. I'll write you and let you know what I'm doing and when I'll be coming back home. Well, I guess I'd better be going."

Lew got back on his horse, rode out the gate, and turned to the left. As he rode, tears fell from his eyes. On his way back towards the big house, Robert also wept. He didn't know if he would ever see his brother again.

Lew rode into town and reported to the Confederate headquarters. He found the captain he had spoken with three days before. The captain was seated at his desk when Lew walked in his office.

"I'm glad that you decided to join us," said the captain, looking up at Lew.

Lew looked him straight in the eye and said, "I don't see where I had a choice."

"No, I guess you don't," said the captain as he leaned back in his chair and laughed.

He then gave Lew an enlistment form to sign and told him to go with the sergeant seated at the desk in the hallway. Lew did what he was told. He signed the paper, walked out of the captain's office, and reported to the sergeant in the hall. He received his unit assignment and a uniform. Then he left Savannah that very same day.

CHAPTER 18

▼

Lew didn't know any of the men in his unit, though most of them were as young as he. Some were even younger. He listened to them talk about killing Yankees, or how they were willing to die for their beliefs. Lew didn't share most of their beliefs, but he never let any of them know it. He kept in his mind the first lesson he had learned in school: "Be known by silence." He realized that the less these men knew about him, the better off he would be. Lew's unit marched for over a week, setting up campsites at night as they went. They were heading somewhere in north Georgia, but no one was told where. The only thing they were told was that they would all soon get the chance to fight for a free and independent South.

When Lew's unit reached the place where they would be fighting, a sergeant named Thomas Monroe asked Lew how well he could shoot a rifle. Lew told the sergeant that he had never shot a riffle in his life. Sergeant Monroe shook his head and laughed at him. Then he assigned him to work with the unit's medical division. He then told Lew that he wouldn't need his horse anymore. He said the troops on the front line needed it more. Even though Lew did not like the fact that his horse was taken away from him, there was nothing he could say or do about it so he reported to the doctor's tent. He was told that he would sleep in a smaller tent right behind it with some of the other soldiers. Lew found the tent and met the other men that were staying there.

The area where they were stationed was beautiful. He learned that it was called Allatoona. There were wide open fields full of wildflowers, pine trees, and a large creek that ran along the edge of the field. Lew often thought to himself how peaceful it was there. Things were fine for about a week. Then all at once, the sense of peace that Lew had been enjoying was destroyed by the reality of the war.

The fighting began and Lew found himself right in the middle of it. His job was to help tend to the wounded when they came in from the battlefield. It seemed like a never-ending task because they kept coming in by the dozens. There was blood everywhere, and the smell was unbearable like the smell of death filling the air. Aside from that, the countless number of dead soldiers was unbelievable. The continuous sound of gunfire and cannons were enough to drive you insane. Then all at once, the fighting would stop for a day or two. On one of the days when the fighting stopped, Lew wrote two letters home. He didn't know if they would reach them or not, but he wrote one to his father, and the other to Robert.

My Dearest Father,

I hope that this letter fines you of good health, and of good spirits. As for myself, I'm trying to deal with the ravages of this horrible war. Besides that, I'm fine and in good health. I'm in Allatoona Georgia, which is about 285 miles northwest of Savannah. The army made me an assistant medic. This I am grateful for, and at the same time appalled. I find myself increasingly appalled by this war. The mere disregard for life is more than anyone should have to bear. I've found myself living in conditions in which no human being should ever have to endure. I see on a daily basis a steady stream of dead and wounded soldiers. This war inflicts pain and suffering on so many people every day. I try my best to help as many as I can. However, I find myself fighting a losing battle. Some I can help, however, the majority I can do nothing for, I just pray that this awful war will be over soon, and I can return home to Woodloe.

Your loving son,
Lew Jones

To Robert he wrote:

My Dearest Brother,

I'm writing to let you, Ada, and the rest of the people on Woodloe know that I'm all right and thinking of you everyday. Give Mama Ada a kiss for me. Robert, you wouldn't believe the kinds of things I've seen. War is more horrible than anyone could ever imagine. I've seen things that makes it hard for me to sleep at night. I find myself not able to eat, and I have lost a large amount of weight. I have never been so afraid in my life. I try my best not to show it. Death is all around me, and I fear that I won't make it back home. I pray everyday that I will. However, if I don't, please take care of Woodloe Plantation, and our father. He is a good man, and he needs your help. You two are more alike then either one of you realize.

Your loving brother,
Lew

CHAPTER 19

▼

On Woodloe things were quiet and sad. With Lew gone off to fight, Master Jones found it hard to concentrate on running the plantation properly and it seemed to be falling apart. He told Ada that he would quickly give Woodloe away just to have his son back with him. The big house fell into disrepair and needed painting badly. The road leading to the house was ragged with ruts that needed to be filled and smoothed out. A few of the windows were broken and the shutters began to fall off. Master Jones could have gone into town to buy new glass for the windows and paint for the house but he wouldn't. In fact, he wouldn't go into town for anything.

Whenever one of his neighbors from down the road or someone from Savannah stopped by the plantation, the only thing they ever talked about was the war. Master Jones didn't care to hear what folks had to say about it because he didn't agree with this war.

The people of Savannah had begun to use Confederate currency. However, Master Jones refused to use it himself. So he didn't sell anything unless the buyer had what he called, "real American money." Such money was soon in very short supply around Savannah because a lot of people had traded it in at the banks for Confederate money. As for the Confederate soldiers who came to Woodloe, they never paid Master Jones for anything that they took. Master Jones told himself that the ruts in the road made it harder for them when they came to steal from him. Not making it easier for them was his way of fighting back.

The slaves went about their work, tending to the fields and preserving the harvest they produced. They stored sacks of rice, and barrows of syrup and rum in several storehouses. Although Master Jones did not go into town himself, he would sometimes hire a neighbor to go in and make trades for him.

Robert recovered completely from the beating he had suffered and kept himself busy working in the fields. Sometimes, at night, he secretly taught some of the other slaves to read and write.

In the past, Master Jones often took walks around the plantation in the evenings, but since Lew's departure he didn't do this anymore. Once he had eaten his supper, he just stayed in the house. On occasion, he and Ada would sit and talk for hours at a time, or he would read one of his many books, and go to bed. He and Robert would talk every now and then, but they never talked about being father and son. Instead, they talked about Lew, or the plantation. Master Jones seemed to want Robert to make sure that things were progressing as they should, and Robert started doing just that. He got Master Jones to think about going to town so they could get the supplies needed to at least paint and repair the house. Everything was fairly easy because everyone on the plantation knew just what to do, and how to do it. They all worked together and helped each other. And they all missed Lew, especially Robert.

Master Jones decided to follow Robert's suggestion and one day went into town for the supplies they needed. While there, he went by the telegram office and found there were two letters from Lew, one addressed to Robert and one to himself. He was very happy to hear from his son. It had been about a month and a half since Lew had left the plantation. Master Jones was beginning to think the worst. Master Jones opened his letter and read it right away. He took Robert's letter back home with him and gave it to Robert. After the first letter, each of them would receive a letter about every two months or so. Master Jones and Robert always looked forward to hearing from Lew. They both knew that as long as they received letters from Lew, he was alright.

Life went on this way for about two years. Then one day in December of 1864, Union soldiers marched into the city of Savannah. They had taken the city, and had captured or killed the Confederate troops that were there. General Grant was said to have given President Abraham Lincoln the city of Savannah as a Christmas gift. Soon after that, the Union soldiers arrived at Woodloe. About sixty of them marched down the long dirt road. They stopped in front of the big house, then all at once turned to face it. They were dressed in blue uniforms with gold buttons down the front. The soldiers called Master Jones outside and asked him some questions. They also questioned some of the slaves. Afterwards, they told Master Jones that the war would soon be over, and that the South was losing. This meant that the slaves would soon be free to come and go as they pleased. Robert asked one of the Union soldiers about Allatoona and learned that some of the worst fighting had taken place there. However, all of the fighting was over now, and the Confederate soldiers there were either dead or captured. This made Robert worry even more than he had at first. He knew there was nothing he could do except pray that Lew was not one of those who had been killed and hope that he would soon come back home.

Shortly after the soldier arrived, Old Jordan became ill. Two men carried him to his cabin and put him to bed. Another went to get Miss Lizzy to see what she could do for him. She looked at the old man and said she could not help him. His time was near. Robert stayed by his bed and wouldn't leave, not to eat, sleep, not for anything. He remembered how Old Jordan had taught him to cook eggs with the ashes from a fire. He remembered how he would ask Old Jordan a thousand questions and Old Jordan would answer every one of them. And he remembered how the old man had watched over him after Isaac had beaten him so badly that he almost died. Old Jordan was like a father to him and the fact that he might die was unacceptable to Robert. Sure, Robert knew that everyone had to die sooner or later, but it couldn't be Old Jordan's time yet.

Old Jordan told Robert that he had something to tell him. Robert said, "Jordan, you know you can tell me anything." Old Jordan told him that he couldn't ever tell anyone what he was about to hear. Robert made a promise that he wouldn't say a word.

"You remember the day Isaac hit me in the mouth with the butt of his whip?" asked Old Jordan. "Well that I could take. But that day he tried to kill you was more than I could stand. You have been like a son to me. Sure, I knew you was Master's child, that didn't matter to me. You made me proud. You were a good boy, and you did what you were told. So it hurt me when Isaac beat you for nothing. Then the day he kicked Ada in the big house, that was the final straw. I could take no more of Isaac. The Master wasn't going to do anything, so I did."

Robert looked into Old Jordan's deep brown eyes and asked, "What do you mean?"

Old Jordan stared back and answered, "Son, no Union soldier killed Isaac. I did. I'm the one that shot him."

Robert sat there for a second or two without saying a word. Old Jordan knew him well. He knew that his mind was racing. He would soon start asking questions. Knowing this, Old Jordan instructed Robert not to ask anything else nor ever talk about it again. Instead, they talked about the happy times on Woodloe and about the people living there. Old Jordan had held most of them when they were babies. They talked about what Robert would do when he was freed. Robert said he wanted to be a teacher. He knew how to read and write, so he wanted to teach. He wanted a little schoolhouse like the one Lew had gone to as a boy. Old Jordan told him that he would make a good teacher. Then he asked Robert to read to him.

"Sure," said Robert, and went home to get his bible.

Robert read to Old Jordan the rest of that day, and long after dark until he fell asleep. Sometime during the night Old Jordan passed away while Robert slept in a chair next to his bed. When Robert woke the next morning, he realized Old Jordan had died in his sleep. The old man was buried that same day in a grave next to the river. Everyone on the plantation attended his funeral. It was a long one that lasted for hours, mostly because everyone wanted to say something about Old Jordan. He had helped so many people in his lifetime. Even though he never married and lived by himself, he had been like a father to a lot of people. They all would miss him dearly.

Robert began to think about what Old Jordan had told him. He had so many unanswered questions in his mind. Where had Old Jordan gotten a rifle? And how long had he had it? Where did he hide it, and why did the Confederate soldiers say that Isaac was killed by a Union soldier's rifle? All of these questions raced through Robert's mind. He decided to clean Old Jordan's house. One of the other slaves could let their oldest son or daughter move in it. This would be decided by putting all of their names in a hat, and pulling one out. Robert cleaned the house from top to bottom. He looked for the rifle but didn't find it. Knowing Old Jordan the way he did, he knew that he would never find it, so he just gave up. Robert told himself that people are not meant to know everything. But he did know one thing. He knew he wished that Lew was there so he could talk with him about everything that was happening.

CHAPTER 20

▼

New Year's day 1865 came on Woodloe Plantation and, besides the letters that Robert and Master Jones had received the year before, there was still no word from Lew. The sky was gray and the trees were all bare. Everyone's spirits were low. It was as if none of them had any energy to do anything except what they absolutely had to on the plantation. There was no laughing or singing. The slaves went about automatically doing their jobs and going back to their cabins each night. The only way you could tell people lived on the plantation after a day's work was by the smoke that would pour from the chimneys of their homes and then disappear into the gray sky. Life on Woodloe went on this way for the whole month of January and into early spring.

Then one day at the beginning of April, news came that after all this time the war had finally ended. The next time soldiers visited Woodloe was to inform Master Jones and the slaves that the end of the war had also brought an end to slavery. Some of them, slaves no more, danced around the plantation as happy as they could be and announced they would soon be leaving. Others said that Woodloe Plantation was their home and they would stay. They all were uncertain about what the future had in store for them. Robert and Ada decided that they would stay. Ada would continue to cook for Master Jones. Robert, on the other hand, wanted to build a schoolhouse, and become a teacher. He didn't know if he would build it on the plantation or somewhere else.

A week after he had heard the news about the end of the war and the end of slavery, Robert decided to take a walk. He walked down the long dirt road towards the arched gate. He walked out the gate and looked down the road that led into town. He felt strange being able to just walk right off of the plantation that way with no one questioning or challenging him. He said to himself, "I guess this is what being free feels like." Then he turned around, went back down the road, and walked into the wildflower field.

As Robert lay in the field he thought about Lew. He gently ran his hand across the tops of some of flowers as he closed his eyes. Laying there in the warmth of the sun, he fell asleep. He barely felt it when something brushed up against the side of him, but he immediately recognized the voice that woke him.

"You hear me Robert? I said don't move. If you do, I'm thinkin' that rattler just might get excited and bite you full of poison."

Without moving his head, Robert looked first at the poisonous diamond-back rattle snake that had crawled halfway onto his chest. Then his eyes rolled to the side and there was Lew, dirty and ragged, standing seven or eight feet away. The rattle snake seemed to be studying Robert's face and deciding where it was going bite him. Robert thought he could hear Old Jordan's voice inside his head, telling him to be still and to hold his breath as steady as he could.

Then he saw Lew crouching down like he was about to jump toward him but he didn't jump. Instead, he started making a strange hissing sound with his throat and a clicking sound with his tongue: "Hissssss tic tic tic! Hissssss tic tic tic!" Robert didn't know what to think of it until he saw the snake turn toward Lew, who kept his eyes directly on it while continuing to make that strange sound. The snake wriggled its fat body straight across Robert's chest. Lew began to step backwards as the snake moved away from Robert and started crawling towards him. When the snaked moved faster, instead of taking another step backward, Lew stepped forward and jumped over the snake to land in front of Robert. The snake kept going off toward the woods.

"Boy, I hope you been doing more than laying around playing with snakes every day," said Lew.

Robert hugged him, and as they hugged they both started to cry. They weren't crying because of pain or sorrow. No, these were tears of joy. While still hugging Lew, Robert said, "Since when you learn how to charm a snake?"

"You learn how to do a lot of things when you have to."

"Yeah, I guess you do, especially if you fightin' in a war. I hope you remembered how to take a bath cause you sure do stink."

Lew, without letting go said, "Yeah, I do don't I," and they both started to laugh.

Robert looked over to where the snake had crawled away and didn't see anything but the early spring wildflowers starting to bloom. He realized how close he had come to being bitten, shook his head, and moved back from Lew.

"Lew I think you just saved my life."

"Yeah? Well since you saved mine from that water moccasin when we was kids, I guess we finally even."

They left the field and walked towards the big house. Some of the newly-freed slaves saw them and started to shout, "Master Lew home, Master Lew home!"

Hearing this, Master Jones came out of the house, ran down the porch steps, and hugged his son. Tears of joy fell from his eyes also.

"How are you father?" Lew asked.

"I've never been better, now that you're back home," Master Jones replied with a big smile on his face.

"Now, let's get you washed up and into some decent clothes." As they all went into the house, Lew walked between Robert and Master Jones, who each had an arm resting across Lew's shoulders. Once inside, Lew went upstairs to his room, Master Jones went into his sitting room, and Robert went into the kitchen to tell Ada that Lew was home. After Lew had washed and changed his clothes, he went downstairs and into the kitchen to see Mama Ada. She started to cry as she hugged him.

"My baby, my baby," she cried as she held his face in her hands. "Sit down and let me get you something to eat."

Lew had lost a lot of weight. Ada said that he was as skinny as a beanpole. Lew ate, then told Ada that he just had to get some sleep because he had been walking off and on for a week. He promised to talk with everyone later.

Lew slept the rest of that day, all that night, and most of the next day.

Finally, he woke up and walked over to his bedroom window. When he looked outside, he saw that a feast had been prepared for him. The tables were set and everyone seemed to be waiting for him to come out. Life on Woodloe Plantation had come full circle and was now back to normal again. Everyone was happy. The former slaves danced, sang, and played banjos. The children played among themselves while adults looked on laughing. When Lew came out of the house, he joined Master Jones and Robert at the head table, with Lew on one side of this father and Robert on the other. All of them, blood kin, enjoyed the feast together.

EPILOGUE

▼

Master Jones lived to a ripe old age of eighty-nine. He enjoyed his final years on Woodloe Plantation and was buried next to his wife and Isaac.

Lew Jones married a woman name Sarah Tillman from Savannah and with her had three children. He named his oldest son Robert and raised all of his children on Woodloe Plantation.

Ada stayed on Woodloe as the head cook. She lived to the age of ninety-six. When she died, she was buried on the plantation in a grave next to Old Jordan.

Robert lived on Woodloe and built a schoolhouse a quarter of a mile from the stone arched gateway of the plantation. He taught both white and black, adults and children, how to read and write. He never married or had children of his own. However, he did spend a lot of time with Lew's children. They all called him Uncle Robert.

978-0-595-45129-6
0-595-45129-2

LaVergne, TN USA
16 April 2010
179480LV00002B/1/A